D1319898

SAY NOTHING

SAY NOTHING

JAMES HANLEY

HORIZON PRESS
NEW YORK
1962

© James Hanley, 1962

First published in the United States in 1962 by
Horizon Press Inc.
Made and printed in Great Britain by
Purnell and Sons, Ltd.
Paulton (Somerset) and London

I

"Who will forgive you, Mrs. Baines?"

Silence.

"*Crawl* up the Cross."

Silence.

"Cry, you bitch, *cry*."

And she cried in the morning that exploded like bombs.

A moment for Winifred, in the town of bells, blue suits, and roast beef. But nothing for Baines. He has no moments.

"Are you damned, Baines?"

Standing back from this, not a part, holder of the wreath. Damned, and done, and done with. There is nothing for Baines, nothing, except the single dream, in the night, and in the dark corner, cradling the day in his head, the one he will walk into, away from the sin, and the nails, and the flesh. If the chain breaks he will rise up and walk out, and on, and on and on. The day rocks in his head. He feels it there, *knows* it there, as he stands motionless, frozen into the silence that is itself frozen. He watches Winifred claw at the grave, and thinks of the flowers that will weigh Tom down. He watches Mrs. Baines. He listens to the sobs.

"Go away, Mrs. Baines."

And she went away, raising her body slowly, clumsily and staggering back, to where he was now, on another Sunday, that is the same as the last, and will be the same on the next.

"Give me the wreath," Winifred said.

7

He gave it, and she did not thank him.

He felt for Mrs. Baines's hand, held it tightly, as he watched, as Mrs. Baines watched him watching.

Winifred's feverish fingers traced the anatomy of grave and Cross.

"You lie on my heart, Tom," Winifred said.

He watched her bend low, then very low, then saw her lie flat, her arms outstretched.

"She will reach out each day until her arms reach his."

"Are you ready, Mr. B.," Mrs. Baines said.

"I am ready, Mrs. Baines."

And they went on watching. Hand clutched hand.

"What are you thinking, Mr. B.?" Mrs. Baines said.

"I dare not say."

"*She* thinks she will break me, Mr. B., but she won't."

Winifred rose, turned, suddenly stiffened, turned again to look, leaned over, as though by some terrible urge she would draw this sleeper from his bed. Then she walked backwards until she heard the heavy, asthmatic breathing of Baines. A moment had ended.

"I'm ready," she said.

"We are ready then," Baines said.

The Baines feet seem to drive into the gravel, as though seeking a purchase, before the leap that will take him out of this, the morning of God's day.

"Ready, Charlie," he called softly, and the moment he did so, *I* moved.

Winifred passed me, Mrs. Baines, Baines. I stood boulder-still.

"*Charlie!*"

And the hand as heavy as a log on my upper arm. "Charlie," as though he were waking me from sleep. "S'time, Charlie."

I turned. And we went along in the same way, in single file, down to the gates of iron. These *clanged*.

I stare into his broad back. I suddenly hurry forward, touch his shoulder.

"Mr. Baines?"

"Yes, Charlie?"

"How extraordinary," I said.

"Nothing is extraordinary, Charlie. Nothing."

And he walked on, and I walked behind him.

Involuntarily it leaped out. "Dreadful," I said.

He swung round. "What's that?"

"Nothing. Nothing at all," I said.

"I am glad of that," he said.

The pilgrimage is over. In single file we moved towards the town where *everything* is North.

There is a street called Baptist Street, and it is in the town that I came to, and the houses are very tight, in a tight town. The doors give the impression of having been closed forever. The curtains on the windows are as stiff and motionless as sentinels. When first I came to it, I stared and stared. Night has the depth of caves, and daylight has no arch. Not in this town that is called Garlston. Baptist Street curled in on its own silence. And I was lost in this town, rootless. Until the evening that I walked up to number seventeen and knocked. The door swung open as clean as a blade. It was as if the person had stood waiting behind it, for me. The voice was a knife.

"Well?"

"Good evening," I said. "I am the new lodger."

"New lodger?"

Neither shadow nor substance, just a voice. The hall lies in a curious half light. I heard a movement, then suddenly saw the woman at the door. She had turned inwards.

"New lodger," she called.

And from the foot of the stairs a man's voice called "new lodger", and from the top of the stairs another voice cried

9

shrilly "new lodger". Then an echo in the hall. "New lodger."

I heard feet on the stairs, a door open and close. I waited. I listened. There was a whisper close to my ear.

"Come."

And the man's voice. "I heard."

And the woman at the door, the knife. "Name?"

"Elston. Charles Elston. You *are* Mrs. Baines?"

"Should I be somebody else then? You wrote?"

"I answered the advertisement in the *Church Gazette*. You asked me to call."

"You had better come in."

I came in. I shall not soon forget the slam of the front door, the key in the lock, the suddenly shot bolt. I thought I was locked in forever.

"This way." And I went that way.

"In here."

"Thank you."

I was in this hall. A green jungle, green walls, green linoleum, green fanlight, green air.

"*Right*."

"*Right*." And I was in the kitchen.

"New lodger," announced Mrs. Baines, and it was like an ultimatum.

She turned sharply. "Name Charles, or just Charlie?"

"Either, Mrs. Baines."

There is something hooded, unsubstantial, about the light in the kitchen, a sort of fog, through which I now heard the thin, thread-like voice of another woman. It was Winifred.

"Evening."

"Good evening," I said.

The man spoke, but the word seemed locked in his teeth. "Nin."

They went out. I was alone with Mrs. Baines.

"Take off your coat, Charlie. Sit down."

"Thanks. I will."

I looked round the kitchen. "It's rather difficult to find rooms in a town these days, Mrs. Baines."

"Difficult to find anything, *really*. Terms cash here. Meals with us. I'll show you your room."

"Thanks."

"This way, Charlie."

I followed her out. She paused for a moment at the foot of the stairs. Then I seemed to be going up, and up, and *up*, but eventually we reached the top. A door knob rattled with great violence.

"This way, Charlie."

I hesitated, but only a second.

"All *right*. Go *in*. Room won't bite, Charlie. Supper at seven."

"Thank you."

Her descent of the stairs was heavy, and seemed headlong. I closed my door.

"Well," I thought, "here I am."

And there I was in a room like a box, a tight little room in the tight town. I stared about. The window was small, and it was barred. It was also locked.

"Nothing can come in here, and nothing can get out." I sat down. A ship's cabin is small, and this was smaller. It contained one iron bed, one chair, a mountainous wardrobe that suffocated the wall. One small table. Red curtains on the window. I pushed at this window. It gave the squeak of an owl, but refused to yield. And the grate. What a pinhead of fire will glow in it. Who could ever have sat by this grate except dwarfs, or perhaps fairies. Over the mantelpiece a picture that seems as big as the wardrobe. An angel in flames.

"Supper."

I stiffened. The voice came to me as out of a void.

"*Coming—thank—*you."

I shut the door and went slowly downstairs. I entered the kitchen.

Immediately a dark cloud arose from a corner, and it turned out to be Mr. Baines, whose name I discovered was Joshua.

"Ah! There you are, Charlie," he said. "Just sit there, s'right."

"Thanks," I said, looked from one to the other of the trinity, and added, "A nice evening."

"Every evening is nice, Charlie," he said, and the bass voice rang out like bells. "Ready, Mrs. Baines?" he asked.

I sat opposite him. Then a voice close to my ear, asked, "Do you live by the Word, Charlie?"

"The Word? . . . Ah! Thanks, Mrs. Baines."

"Eat, Charlie. Sit down now, Mrs. Baines."

"Yes, Mr. B.," she replied, and I was quick to notice the loud creak of the chair as she did so.

The bell-like voice was now closer to my ear.

"In this house we live by the Word," said Baines.

"Time now," said Winifred, and I alerted at once.

"I *know* when it is time, and *don't tell* me, Winifred," he said.

The subdued light falls upon us all, and in a moment Baines is vast, as he picks up the Book, chain and anchor, Master and mystery, and with his rolling bass he lifts up the words from the mauled pages, from behind the prison of ink. In a foggy kitchen they rise like stars.

"But his word was in mine heart as a burning fire shut up in my bones. And I was heavy with fore-bearing. And I could not stay. For I heard the defaming of many. Fear on every side. Report, say they, and we will report it. All my familiars watched for my halting, saying, 'Peradventure he will be enticed, and we shall prevail against him. And we will take revenge on him.' "

Baines paused, to ahem, to cough.

"Tell us we pray thee, for what cause this evil is upon us. What is thine occupation? Whence comest thou? What is thy country, and of what people art thou?"

The words rolled deep into the silence. Then suddenly he said in my ear, "*Eat.*"

I resumed my meal.

"He speaks but into a desert, Charlie."

They do not ask me who I am, nor what I am? And now I am beginning to wonder who they are. The clock ticked as heavy as feet. The parrot called in gibberish.

"Cover him up, Mrs. Baines," Mr. Baines said.

"*Very* well."

"I am glad of that," Joshua said, then turned to me. "Have you finished?"

I jumped. "*Me?* Oh—why *yes*—of course—thanks."

"Clear away, Mrs. Baines," he said.

The chairs creaked, the crockery rattled. The women departed. The door closed almost silently behind them.

"You are new in a town, Charlie?"

"I am indeed."

"I am old in a town, Charlie," said Baines, and the words seemed *dragged* from the tongue. And he continued.

But I am not listening, just looking about me. I am trying to think of a word that would match this house, and this hour, this kitchen, and this man. And the departed Mrs. Baines.

"You never enquired as to where I came from, Mr. Baines," I said. "Nor did your wife."

13

"I never ask anybody where he comes from, Charlie," and he wiped his mouth with the back of his hand.

"But I'm not the first lodger you've had?"

"And you won't be the last, Charlie. You've been shown your room?"

"I have."

"And there is one other room upstairs, Charlie, and it is ours."

"Of course."

He leaned close, was suddenly confiding. "I'm a failure, Charlie," he said.

"Oh, I'm sorry to hear that, Mr. Baines."

"Have no will, Charlie."

I made no comment. I just looked at Baines, the failure, the will-less one. This confidence is un-asked for, is too sudden.

"Mind my pipe?" he said.

"Not at all. Indeed, I——"

"I'm in nails," Baines said.

"Nails? Oh yes."

"At Lawlers."

"Oh yes."

And Baines was close again. "Hammering in, Charlie, hammering down. Hammer in my head. At *night—dream*—often dream—and the hammering, the *hammer* . . ."

"Yes, of course. I do understand, Mr. Baines," and wondered if I did.

"In a town, Charlie, the days are full of feet, heavy with them, and the hammering . . ."

"I *do* understand," I said.

What else could I say? Locked in this place, staring at this man, securely hidden inside his own giant endeavour of flesh and bone.

"Every day the same, Charlie."

14

"I know."

"Every *life*, Charlie."

The eyes are of an almost puppy blue, the hands like hams. The chest *thrusts*.

His voice was suddenly sharp. "You know the rules?"

"Mrs. Baines has informed me about everything," I said. "Meals with the family. *Cash* down. *You* rise early, retire early."

"S'right."

The door opened, and Mrs. Baines came in. A little bent, tense, silent. She sat down, opposite the failure. Would she speak? I waited. I edged a little away from Baines's breathings. Who would be the first? I wondered. The woman sat tight, hands in her lap, and stared into the fire. She clutches the chair arm, her shoulders huddle. Life crouches in Mrs. Baines. I looked across at her. Her eyes are half-closed, and I think they will soon shut tight, as by some pressure that even now seems to cling to the eyelids. The room smothers, drowns in smoke from the Baines pipe. I wanted to cough, but dared not. I dreaded to break a silence that seemed at once law and vigil, elected, vowed. I was startled when he spoke.

"Been a nice day."

"Very nice," I said.

"It was nice *yesterday*, and I know it'll be nice to-morrow," Mrs. Baines said.

"I'm sure it was," I replied.

But I wasn't sure and met her penetrating eyes. She then turned to Baines. "What did Crawley say?"

"Nothing," replied Mr. Baines.

"Perhaps he will to-morrow, Mr. B."

"Perhaps."

"You think he'll keep his word, Mr. Baines?"

"Who asked you to *speak*?"

"I'm sorry," Mrs. Baines said, and truly looked it. Her head lowered.

For a moment I shut my own eyes. Where will they go on Sunday? How far? For what? Why? The smoke from the pipe curled upwards, fanned outwards. Through the clouds I can see the still pair. How strange. How suddenly silent. What ritual is this?

"Satisfied?" The word shot like a bullet from Baines's mouth.

It is like a dream. I sat up quickly, hardly realizing that he was addressing me.

"What's that?"

"Your *room*, Charlie," he said. "Satisfied with it? If not, say so. Soon get somebody else. Space is like gold, isn't it, Mrs. Baines?"

"Like gold, Charlie," she said, "like real gold."

Abruptly I rose to my feet, pushed in the chair, turned to Mrs. Baines. "I think I'll go up now," I said. "If you'll excuse me—I have some work to do."

Joshua rose, moved towards the door with me. "Where will you work in a town, Charlie?"

"I shall be studying the law with Greele and Grimes," I said. "I expect you've heard of them. Solicitors in Dove Place—they——"

"Student then?" said Mrs. Baines, and she turned in her chair.

I smiled. "You could call it something like that," I replied.

Joshua faced me. "Student of *what*?"

"The *law*."

"*That?*"

"That."

"Only one law really, Charlie, and it is in the Word," Mrs. Baines said.

"Yes, yes, of course, Mrs. Baines."

"And work is salvation," announced Mr. Baines.

"*Indeed* it is," I said.

"You locked the windows, Mr. B.?"

"They are locked, Mrs. Baines," he said, and the words fell like stones.

"The doors?"

"I'll just look again," Joshua said.

"Don't look if you've already *done* it."

Baines exploded. "I *have* done *it*."

"All right, all *right*."

The words appear to have hung for too long on the fringe of nerves. Mrs. Baines got up, still bent, and walked stiffly towards the door, fascinating in her departure.

"Who has died, Mr. Baines?"

I got up, lit a cigarette.

"Sit, Charlie, sit," he said.

I sat. "Who?"

"Her first husband."

"I *am* sorry."

"Not to worry, Charlie, it's a time ago."

Mrs. Baines returned, stood, and surveyed us both.

"Are *you* coming, Mr. B.?" she said.

"I'm coming," he said.

The silence that followed seemed too sudden, as was the voice that broke it. "Are you there?"

I turned right round, I wondered. Who had spoken? From where?

The Baines pair had stiffened, and now stood there, motionless.

"We're here!" shouted Joshua.

"Did you get the wreath then, did *you*?"

Mrs. Baines spoke. "We did then."

"At Duthies?"

Another woman, a thin, thread-like voice. But from which room?

"Tell her, Mr. B."

"We got it. S'all right then, our Winifred."

"It'll be cold to-morrow, Mr. B. Feel it."

"Does it matter?"

"It *might*."

A frantic call. "Where *is it*?"

"In the *sink*. Where else then?"

An awkward moment, and no way out. I felt the Baines eyes on me.

"S'orl right, Charlie," Mrs. Baines said. "Not to worry."

"I'm not."

"Sright then."

Baines took out his watch and checked it by the big clock in the corner.

"To-morrow is Sunday, Mrs. Baines. *Rest*."

"*She* won't."

"She never does. You *know* that."

"You are going away to-morrow, Mrs. Baines?" I enquired. She looked at Baines. "Tell him."

"We go out to Garlan Road to-morrow, Charlie. S'in the country. Know the country then?"

"Which country?"

"Up here, Charlie?"

"Afraid I don't."

"Like to *come*, Charlie?" asked Mrs. Baines.

"Can I think about it?"

"You'll do as you want to do, Charlie. I am going up, Mr. B. And don't forget anything."

"I won't," he said.

"Good night, Mrs. Baines," I said.

"Good night then."

The door closed. I was alone with the failure.

"Sit back then, Charlie. S'orl right."

I took Mrs. Baines's chair.

"Thank you. Who is Winifred?"

"Her sister."

"Is she——?"

"In the front parlour, Charlie. *Her* room."

"She's had no supper."

"Eats alone. She'll have hers when we go up then."

I looked into the fire, closed my eyes. Where will they go on Sunday? How far? For what? The smoke poured from the Baines pipe, and through the cloud I looked at the man without will. How strange, how silent, and the other one, and the shouting from room to room. What ritual is this? Shall I feel my way in? Break the ice?

Instead of which I moved to the door.

"If you'll excuse me, Mr. Baines. I'll go up now. Rather tired."

The arm came out, the hand now heavy on my shoulder. "Sit, Charlie. Her *first* husband," he said.

"I see." But do I? And under my breath, I exclaimed, "*Do* I?"

Baines pounced. "What's that, Charlie?"

"Nothing, nothing. You were saying, Mr. Baines——"

"She loved Tom from the skin of the soles of his feet to the tip of his hair."

"She did?"

"Winifred. Said it. Her arm's round nothing these days, Charlie, nothing. 'Cept that place out there," and the big hand shot up, the finger pointing. "Arm *that* far, sort of hangs there, *dead*."

"How extraordinary, Mr. Baines," I said.

"S'nothing extraordinary, never was."

"You like having lodgers?"

"Mrs. B. likes having money."

"Where does Winifred sleep?"

"*Told* you. Out there!"

"Oh!"

"Front parlour. Likes being there. Likes being alone. Always talks about going away somewhere, never does, *really*, 'cept Sundays. She's like that, Charlie. Odd."

"I see."

"I am going to bed now, Charlie. I rise early, but you'll get up when you want to."

He rose from the chair, massive, then leaned forward, and again the hand sought my shoulder.

"Not to worry a bit, Charlie. S'right."

"Of course not."

"I'm glad of that," he said.

And so was I. I wanted nothing so much as to leave this kitchen, go up to my room, sit down, and think about things. About that wreath, about Winifred, about this odd house where the Word soars, and is triumphant.

"I'm off now," I said.

"S'right. Just going to check things up then, Charlie. Mrs. B. worries if everything's not shut down fast."

He went to the door, and I followed behind him, out into the green hall.

"Wait," he said, listening, his head turned to the window. The noise was sudden, like thunder, and then like that of armies.

"What on earth is that?" I asked, and I came back into the kitchen.

"Come and look, Charlie," he said, and I followed him to the window. This shot up.

"There it is, Charlie. The lot. Know it all. Come and look then," and he pressed my head out of the window. "See? See that?"

And I looked into Baptist Street.

"Hear it then? See it? The world, Charlie. Coming home. Home from the pictures, dances, dogs, devils, dream palaces. They *love* it. The lot of it."

I was glad I pulled my head in for the window went down with a crash. He locked it, then turned away with a gesture of utter disgust.

"Know it *all*."

"I must go up now, Mr. Baines," I said.

"Just going to see as everything's all right, Charlie," he said.

And again I heard the window catches, the bolts. Nothing will get in and nothing will get out.

"Good night."

"Wait!"

"Well?"

The arm on my shoulder, the appeal, the gentle pushing backwards, and then I was in the chair again, and the bed seemed much farther away.

"You like being in the world, Charlie?"

He looked at me with great seriousness, the great frame seemed locked in concentration. His hands pressed on my knees. "Well?"

I laughed. I had to. "Question hardly arises, Mr. Baines. I'm *in* it."

The eyes pinned me to the chair.

"I often think about it," he said. "Like a cup of tea?"

"Really, no. Had enough. I must get upstairs."

Deaf, or wholly indifferent to my reply, he continued.

"Was a man came to me on my bench to-day, and he said to me, 'Baines, I really don't know how you can keep going on, nails, nails, nails.' Made me think about my life then, Charlie, and I thought how far away from my life I'd like to get, very far away, so I said to him, sort of desperate like, 'I *can't*,' and he said, sharp-like, '*Don't* if you don't want to then,' and walked away, like me hammering them in give him an ache——" He paused. "You *are* listening, Charlie?"

"I am."

21

"Queer thing life. Man can be an angel to one, a bastard to another."

"I *must* get off to bed," I said.

"Day before yesterday, Charlie, in the evening it was, I was sitting just there, where you are now, just sitting, thinking of nothing much really, and then I heard a voice. *There!* Just there. Mrs. B. was gone out, very unusual with her, and I was just loving it by the fire that's never been out since her dad died, never, Charlie. Kitchen's like hell in the summer-time. No matter. Well then, I just heard words, and they never come up out of anybody's throat, never. Fact."

He leaned over me, dropped his voice.

"It was the house, *talking*."

"Talking? The *house*?"

"S'right, Charlie."

"How *very* extraordinary."

"And it said to me, 'You should get up, Mr. Baines, and you should go out, and you should walk far into the day that will be long, and white with snow, and you should walk on, and on and on, always hoping, away from the feet, and the flesh, and the sin.'"

"How odd. What happened?"

The big body moved backwards and forwards in the chair, cradled in intensity.

"I just thought of that day, Charlie, I did, *really*, could sort of *feel* it, the freshness of it, the endlessness of it, that's what I liked best, the endlessness, and I felt *drawn* towards it, away from this house, and this kitchen, and the women in it. Strange, too, Charlie, but I thought I heard a chain *break*."

"Will you walk away into a long day, Mr. Baines?"

"How does one ever know *what* one will do. Sometimes everything's odd, *strange*——"

"How very peculiar."

"Them words lie in my head, Charlie. Like drowned men."

22

"But it was a dream. Only a dream, Mr. Baines," I said.

"Perhaps it was, *really*, but it was lovely, *lovely*."

"The flesh, and the Word, and the Dream. Perhaps they all drown," I thought.

"Sure you won't have that cup of tea then?"

"Almost certain."

I stared at Baines, huge, concentrated, earnest. Perhaps what is locked in may yet come out.

"Nothing's ever what you expect it to be, Charlie, nothing. When first I come to this house, I said to myself, I said, here is my kingdom. Here is the first day in a lovely little house. I could see my life fold well in it, Charlie. I even thought of the promise to come, thought how the day'd be there sudden, and I'd load it with joy. Fact. But we didn't. No. Nothing's like what you want. S'fact." The voice was sad.

"Your day may come."

"You really think so, Charlie?"

I offered him a smile, got up, moved to the door.

"You may go to bed now, Charlie, and so may I."

Something made me pause, fingering the door knob.

"All *right*, Charlie."

The words were like fists. I went slowly up, Baines behind me. And then I forced it out.

"Good night, Mr. Baines."

I could almost *feel* the weight, the burden of Baines behind me. Then his door closed. My own clicked. I sat down on the bed. I was glad to. It had been a strange, unexpected conversation. I began to undress. I could hear the man of nails moving about in the next room, as small, and as tight as my own. I even imagined the huge shadow of Baines toppling its height. I lit a cigarette and switched off the light. I lay in the darkness, listening. The floorboards creaked.

"Has *she* gone in then, Mr. Baines?"

"Not yet, Mrs. B. Not yet."

One boot thudded to the floor, and then the other.

"And don't *clump*, will you, Mr. B. The clumping that goes on in this house. And wind the clock."

"Very well," and a sigh as vast as his frame.

I thought of those "good nights". How good?

"I have something to say, Mr. B."

"You always have something to say."

And he is in nails, I told myself. Hammering them in, hammering them down, wearing out days in the tight town. But hammering them into what? Into who? In a moment this room is full of chairs, tables, coffins, sins, failures, regrets, leaps, endeavours, and silences. What strange catalogue lies behind Baines? The sound of heaving breathings was unnerving. These walls seem made of paper, and at any moment they might blow away.

"Window in Charlie's room won't open, Mrs. B."

"Tell him to push it."

"He has."

"Tell him to push it again, Mr. Baines."

"He has. *Said* so."

"Had to be shut tight that time, Mr. B. You *know* that. Other bugger couldn't *breathe* with it open."

"You *bitch*."

"There," Joshua said. "I *knew* it. She's there. Listening again."

"Isn't she always listening then?"

"Must have gone in for her supper now, Mrs. B."

"Must have then."

"Damn you," and the shout echoed through the house.

A door opened and closed.

"There, Baines. She's gone in now to her supper."

"Sometimes I'm sorry for her, Mrs. B."

"Put a candle in her skull anytime and he's there. *Bound* to be. Roaming."

"I am sorry for her, Mrs. B."

"You *said* that."

"Why do you *do* it, Mrs. Baines?"

"Because she thinks I wouldn't."

"We do anything at our peril, Mrs. Baines, and there's no mercy around. *You* know that. Last night, Mrs. B., I said to myself, 'I think we are damned.' "

"Did you, Bainesy, then?"

"Sometimes when I am closest to myself, Mrs. Baines, I am *most* afraid."

"If only we knew what we wanted, Mr. B. At the right time."

"S'right."

"And *now*, *I* have something to say."

"What then?"

"You went out."

"I know I did."

"Last night."

"I said I did, didn't I?"

"I heard you get up. You said nothing to me, Mr. Baines."

"Nothing, Mrs. B., nothing."

"But you went out."

"Yes. I went out."

"Why?"

"I don't know."

"You *must* know."

"I went up to the top of the street."

"What for?"

"I don't *know*. I just went out. That's all, Mrs. Baines."

"Not a word from you, Bainesy, not a sound. And you did it once before. Didn't you?"

"I came back."

"You came back last time, Mr. B."

"I came back this time, Mrs. Baines."

"Were you running away from me?"

"I went to the top of the street, stood there a few minutes, then come back again."

"Were you running *away*?"

"No."

"Are you sure?"

"Just stood there thinking, then come home again."

"Can't you think here then, can't you? Leaving me alone with that one. *You* know which side your bread's buttered. You know you have a roof over your head. I don't starve you. You were going to go, Bainesy, I know it, *feel* it, a woman knows."

"No. I swear by the Book I'd never leave you, Mrs. Baines. And never leave you alone with *her*. Never."

"You get your bellyful here any time, you get your sleep, you have *me* any time you want, and who'd ever want *you* anytime, well who? I know what you are and what you're not. *I* know about your dreams, Mr. B."

"You *bitch*. You still talking about me then, are you?"

I sat up and switched on the light. The harsh voice tore up the stairs.

"She's still listening, stood at the bottom of the stairs."

The Baines' door opened. "Go to bed, Winifred, go to *bed*!" Baines cried down the stairs.

"Got the other bugger on the brain, Bainesy. You know that."

"Go to sleep, our Winifred."

And the door closed again. The floor creaked, and then the bed.

"Did *he* have to come here, Mrs. B.?"

"Who then?"

"Charlie."

"We want the money, Mr. B. Who knows how long you'll last."

"She cried yesterday."

"She's always crying."

"It's sad, Mrs. B."

"Everything's sad. Think of a day when you're nothing, Mr. Baines. *Nothing*."

"I think of that."

"And go on thinking of it."

"I do."

"All *right* then."

"Let a day end, Mrs. Baines. Will you? Let it die."

"Could have had him if she wanted, and she didn't."

"*You* had him."

"Well then?"

"Mrs. Baines. For the love of Christ. Cannot the dead sleep then?"

"Always handy for you, Mr. B. Isn't He?"

"I can't help what I have in my head."

"And that's not much, Bainesy, and the world knows it."

"Shall the day end then? *Now?*"

"But you won't leave me, Bainesy, will you?"

"I won't leave you."

"Never."

"Until the end."

"The end."

A momentary silence.

"Sometimes I am . . ."

And like a needle into the darkness. "You are *what*, Mrs. Baines?"

Silence.

"Well then?"

Silence.

"*Well*, then?"

"Nothing, Bainesy, nothing."

27

The bass voice presses in, presses down. "You *have* had what you wanted, Mrs. B. You *know* that. You have *had* it. From *her*."

"I'm only what I *am*, Bainesy, you know that."

"*I* know."

"Who can help his flesh?"

"Who can?"

"Sometimes, Mrs. B., I am tired of giving, and I am sick of giving——"

"Are you, Bainesy?"

"I am."

"Move up."

"I am moved up."

"All right. Don't *shout*."

"But you won't ever leave me, Bainesy, will you? Promise then?"

"I'm always promising."

"Imagine being alone with that one."

"Imagine it."

"D'you think he's listening?"

"Who's listening, who?"

"Him in the next room."

"Doubt it, Mrs. B. He's young. Sleep just *drags* them down. Does it matter if he does?"

"Listen."

"I am. I always listen, Mrs. B."

"You're sorry for her, aren't you, Bainesy?"

"I——"

"You're sorry for *her*?"

"Sometimes I'm sorry for myself, Mrs. Baines."

"Fancy."

"And now," Joshua said, "now——"

"Yes, Bainesy, yes," suddenly anxious, and a warmth in the voice.

"At the very last moment, Mrs. Baines, we have to forgive. Shall we——"

"So odd that we forgot, Bainesy, so very odd," Mrs. Baines said.

"I am glad I haven't."

The whole house seemed to tremble, as one after the other they left the bed. Later, the words beat into the silence, and I knew they had knelt down.

"Come unto me all ye that are heavy burdened, and I will refresh you."

Mrs. Baines spoke slowly, concernedly, her voice charged with the moment.

"Ah!" exclaimed Joshua. "*His* words. *What* a fountain."

Then slowly, and together, "We thank thee for what thou hast vouchsafed to us this day."

A pause and then, "Amen."

A sigh, and a struggle to rise. The loud tick of the clock, and the groan of the bed.

"Good night, Mrs. B."

"Good night," she said.

"To-morrow," I thought, "there is some terrible duty to be done. Who will wake first? The parrot?"

2

God's day. The morning exploded. The bells of the world rang in Baptist Street. I sat up, listening to the clanging.

"Of *course*. Sunday."

It was still dark and I began fumbling for the light switch.

"Good Lord! Not eight o'clock yet."

I lay down again.

"*Char*lie!"

The sound came up like a wave, and it was unmistakable.

"Yes?"

The air itself seemed to tinkle like a bell. I covered my head with the sheet.

"*Char*—lie!"

"Damn!"

I jumped out of bed.

"Ye—es. Who is that?" and I stood shivering at the door.

And the foghorn from the bottom of the stairs. "Only me, Charlie. Breakfast."

"Sorry. Down in a minute. Thanks for calling me."

"We never allow anything to go cold in this house, Charlie."

"Yes—yes—of course. Coming down in a tick," I shouted.

"Don't forget then."

I knew I wouldn't. It was a warning. I began to dress. Below, the door slammed.

"I thought Sunday was the day of rest," I said to myself, groping about in the new day.

"Are *you* coming down then, Charlie?"

"Coming."

This second call made me feel a member of the family, at once.

I rushed downstairs and opened the kitchen door, and the first thing that met my eye was Baines. He was in his accustomed place, and dressed in stiffest black.

"Here I am," and I fully expected Baines to say that he was glad of that. "Where do I wash?"

"Back kitchen," he said, not looking at me.

I stared at Mrs. Baines. She was bent over the hob, looking hot, and very earnest, as she stirred a pot.

"My things?"

"S'all in the back, Charlie," she said. "Everything."

"Thanks."

The light in the back kitchen shone pale yellow from a naked bulb.

"My things" I found neatly piled on the shelf over the sink. I began my ablutions. Nothing outside the small window save the banked-up darkness of the winter morning. I then returned to the kitchen and sat down. Mrs. Baines was already waiting.

"Sorry I was late. My watch stopped," I said and looked at Mr. Baines. He sat there, erect, arms folded, leaning heavily on the table edge. There was no answer.

"We are ready, Bainesy," she said.

"Where's Winifred?" I asked.

A baleful stare from Mrs. Baines.

"I said ready, Mr. B."

"Very well," he said, and picked up the Book.

"There is one that is alone," began Baines, "and he hath not a second; yea, he hath neither son nor brother; yet is there no end of all his labour, neither are his eyes satisfied with riches. For whom then, saith he, do I labour, and

deprive my soul of good? This also is vanity, yea, it is a
sore travail. Two are better than one, because they have a
good reward for their labour. For if they fall the one will
lift up his fellow, but woe to him that is alone when he
falleth, and hath not another to lift him up. Again, if two
lie together then they have warmth, but how can one be
warm alone? And if a man prevaileth against him that is
alone, two shall withstand him, and a three-fold cord is not
quickly broken."

He paused, ahem-ed, coughed. He slowly raised his head
and looked steadily at us both.

"Keep thy foot when thou goest to the house of God."

"Amen," Mrs. Baines said.
"Amen," I said.
"Eat your breakfast, Charlie," Joshua said, and I fell
to it.
We ate in silence, and nothing disturbed save the clanging
bells.
"We are going out, Charlie," Mrs. Baines announced.
"Oh yes."
"But you'll do whatever you want to do."
"Charlie said he'd come."
"*Did* you, Charlie?"
"When? Where?"
"Garlan Road. There's some nice trees out there, and the
quiet's lovely," Mrs. Baines said.
Should I go? Shouldn't I?
"Well, Mrs. Baines, I don't really know, I mean—I can't
remember saying I would, is it——"
And then a snub: "Don't if you don't want to."
"Actually I have some studying to do."

32

"Oh," she exclaimed. "I *see*."

"That," exclaimed Baines.

"That, Mr. Baines," I replied.

"Charlie will do what he wants to, Mrs. Baines."

"I told him that."

"I *know* you did."

"Well?" she said.

"Perhaps another time. I could——"

"The quiet's lovely there, Charlie," said Baines.

His expression completely disarmed me.

"Oh, all right then," begrudgingly, "I'll come if you want me to."

"Do you want to then?"

"Yes."

"Settled then, Mrs. Baines."

"Our parrot, Charlie, will say the Lord's Prayer for you if you want it to——"

"Indeed! How clever of it, Mrs. Baines."

She suddenly rose, held Baines with her eye. "And you go upstairs at once, Mr. B., and change that *awful* tie."

"Very well."

The moment he left the kitchen, she sat down again.

"Shall I ask her, Charlie?"

Bewilderment sets in. "What's that, Mrs. Baines, I don't quite——"

"She'll say it if I ask her," she said.

"Not now. Another time. Isn't Winifred having any breakfast?"

"Having it now, Charlie. Be out in a minute then. Eats Sunday dinner *here*, Charlie," thumping the table. "Bainesy and me rests always, Sundays."

"*Rests?*"

"Sright," she said.

I could hear the loud squeak of the Baines boots on the

stairs. When he came in, Mrs. Baines was already standing at the cage talking to the bird in a low voice. She seemed determined that it would do its duty.

"Come along, dear," coaxing, gently rocking the cage.

"Leave her, Mrs. Baines. You know she has moods, Sundays."

"I'm going upstairs to get ready," she said, and left us. I turned to Baines.

"How far is it?"

"Not far."

"Do you——"

"It's getting on time, Mrs. Baines," he called.

"I know that."

"Mr. Baines."

"Well, Charlie, what then?"

"Is Winifred going?"

"Oh, yes."

And after a pause, "We await her pleasure, as they say, Charlie."

"Does she never come in here at all?"

"Only when she wants to, Charlie, but most often she don't want to. That's it, you see."

But I didn't see, and we sat on, waiting for Mrs. Baines. I thought of Winifred.

"Is she——"

"She'll be out when she's ready," he said.

"If I go with them," I asked myself, "what shall I see? What corner shall I turn?"

"Ready!"

I knew at once that it was Winifred. She was in the hall, waiting.

"I wonder what she's like," I asked myself, and then Baines nudged me, saying in my ear, "Ready now then, Charlie."

"Won't be a tick," I said and dashed into the hall.

34

And there, stood behind the front door, was Winifred. Tall, very thin, stiff as a guardee, waiting. I dashed up the stairs, collected hat, coat and scarf.

"That you, Bainesy?"

"It's *me*," I said.

"*She* there then?"

"She is."

"Come when I'm ready."

Slowly I went downstairs. Baines was in the hall, standing by the kitchen door. Winifred had not moved. Mrs. Baines came down.

"Ready then," Baines said. Winifred opened the door, and stepped down into the street.

"Right, Charlie," said Baines, following Mrs. Baines into the street.

They stood for a moment looking at each other, as I shut the door behind me.

"Our Winifred," Baines said. "New lodger, Winifred."

She turned and looked at me. I have never seen so tense an expression.

"Good morning then," she said.

"Good morning, Winifred," I replied.

"And you get going," she said, giving Mrs. Baines a gentle prod in the back.

Winifred, too, is dressed in black. Mrs. Baines walked on, Winifred behind her, Baines following. I took up the rear. A strange procession down the silent street. Not a door opened, not a curtain moved. Once only Winifred turned round, fastened her eye on me, then continued on her way. Her look was penetrating, and it induced in me a certain shyness, a feeling of bewilderment, and curiously enough I was half wanting to smile. And yet I felt that I dared not. There is something in the atmosphere that restrains. Should I catch up with Baines, walk beside him? And all the time my eye holds the tall, thin woman who presses steadily on behind Mrs. Baines. Once, when Mrs. Baines veered sharply to the right, Winifred quickly moved. I stared into that thin back. I thought of Winifred as hound and hunter. I increased my pace. When I was just behind him I spoke.

"I should have thought you'd lie in on a morning like this, Mr. Baines."

He did not turn, but replied casually, "One does what one has to do, Charlie."

"May I ask about——?"

"*Ask*."

"It was really about Mrs. Baines's first husband."

"Well then?" And it was like a shot from a gun.

"Was he?"

"Used to lodge here, Charlie. Was Winifred's intended. Night she was trying on her wedding dress, help of Mrs. Carles, he was *took*——"

"Took?" I pressed forward. "Took?"

"Into Mrs. Baines's bed, Charlie."

"No—good——"

"What's that then, Charlie?"

"How extraordinary," I said.

In single file we turned the corner.

"How far is it?"

"Not far then," and he tramped on doggedly, his right hand deep in his coat pocket, the other holding on to the wreath that draped his shoulder like a lifebuoy. A lady and gentleman passed us by without even a glance.

"Early mass, Charlie," called Baines over his shoulder, a remark that did not seem important to me, not at *that* moment. My whole concentration is upon what moves ahead of me, this odd assembly for Garlan Road.

"Why do they do this? And at this unforgivable hour of the morning?"

36

I shut my eyes for a moment, half wondering if, when I opened them, the Baines party would have vanished. But they were still there, determined upon the task to be done. Suddenly I caught up with him again.

"Mr. Baines."

"Can't stop, Charlie, catching a bus then."

And after that we accelerated mercilessly. The bells have ceased. I think of mass commenced, of a sudden silence, broken only by the rhythmic sound of Baines's boots. How long shall we walk? How far? And as though he had sensed my thoughts, he called back to me, "Catching a bus, Charlie, at Lorne Road."

"Oh!"

Mrs. Baines seems well ahead, striding out as though she must, as if something more powerful than herself drew her relentlessly towards the gate, and the tomb, and the man in it. And Winifred is always behind her, and nothing is more certain than that. I stare at this tall figure, that erect back, those resolute feet, and I think only of an iron will.

The party halted as one.

"Here we are then, Charlie," Baines said, and for the first time turned round.

Nobody spoke. In a moment all four of us appeared to be looking in different directions, as though suddenly subjected to the harsh glare of an unexplainable embarrassment. And at the same time I heard the sound of the approaching bus. It pulled up with a loud screeching of brakes.

We climbed aboard. The bus moved off. We were the only occupants. Winifred chose to sit alone, slumped heavy in her seat. Mrs. Baines sat alone in the seat in front of her. Baines sat on the other side, and myself behind him. The bus grinds its way through the silent streets. And a decidedly cold bus, as Baines had warned, its windows covered with a thin mist. Occasionally the driver turned to look at us. Baines is pressed hard against the window, a giant finger and thumb patiently rubbing on the glass.

"How far?" I asked myself.

This surely is the region of the incommunicable. I can only look, and go on looking, from one to the other of this strange trio. Willed by weakness? By strength? Something made me look towards the man of nails.

"What really happened, Mr. Baines?" under my breath.

Just audible, and it found its way into the Baines ear. He leaned forward, gripped the seat with one hand.

"What happened, what?"

"To him."

He leaned further still, said quietly, "He just died, Charlie." Shall I go further?

"Of what, Mr. Baines?"

And in the same hushed tone, he said, "Doctor said as it was just a shift of the liver, Charlie, but you know what *they* are. Pneumonia, *I* thought, always will, Charlie, and the coughing out of him, the *coughing*, even in his sleep—he——"

The bus stopped. The conductor came on. One after another we said good-morning. The driver got down, came round to us.

"S'here," he said.

"Lorne Road, Charlie," Baines said.

When I turned round I found that Winifred and Mrs. Baines had already left the bus. And they were not waiting for anybody.

"Right, Charlie," his hand on my arm.

"They're in a hurry," I said.

He made no reply. And now I wanted to laugh again, but dared not.

We hurried on after the party. I thought of Baines's dream of that day, of going on and on. Then Winifred stopped, waited for us. Mrs. Baines went on. "Wait then," cried Joshua.

In single file again, towards the gates. Winifred halted, swung round, stared at Mrs. Baines.

"Go on, *you*," she said and Mrs. Baines went on. She did not look at us.

We passed through the iron gates. I was struck by the Baines gesture as he opened them; it made the whole thing seem like an occasion. Our feet sank into the deep gravel. In the still air I heard a distant tinkling of glass, the sound of metal against stone. I looked to the right. A man was already at the end of the row, tending a grave. On we went. There is no word that would quite describe this walk, this atmosphere. Winifred halted. Baines looked at me.

"Don't mind waiting, Charlie?"

I shook my head, and slowly retreated to the distance of respect.

And at *last*, the Duthie wreath changed its position. It came slowly down from the Baines shoulder. He now raised it in the air, holding it a little way from him. He turned again.

"Sure?"

"I don't mind."

I looked at these people, graven into the island of silence. I looked at the grave, the marble-surrounded tomb, the stone cross, the mound of dead flowers. They stand motionless, they stare. When Winifred knelt down Baines drew back a little, and Mrs. Baines, her head bowed, remained close to the cross. Baines held out the wreath to the full length of his arms, as though he could no longer stand the strong scent of the flowers. He seemed a little out of it, not a part. Then Winifred swung round.

"Give it me."

Baines went forward and gave her the wreath. She held this tightly to her, like a shield. And the words came slowly, distinctly, on the frozen air:

"You lie in my heart, Tom, and always will."

39

She laid it down, and it never occurred to her to remove the dead flowers that now lay beneath it. Mrs. Baines came forward, knelt.

"I am sorry for my sin," Winifred said.

"I am sorry for my sin," Mrs. Baines said.

"Say it again," Winifred cried.

"I am sorry for my sin."

And then a gentle screech, "*Again*."

"I am sorry——"

"Who will ever forgive *you*, Mrs. Baines?" Winifred said.

Joshua suddenly drew back, his thick boots driving into the gravel. He held his black bowler stiff in his hand.

"Crawl up the cross, Mrs. Baines," Winifred said.

The silence that followed was momentary, but intense.

"Cry, you bitch, *cry*," Winifred said, and a hand fell on Mrs. Baines like a claw. "Go on, cry."

What followed was embarrassing, and humiliating. Mrs. Baines gave a slight jerk of her body, her shoulders slumped, her head fell slowly forward, and suddenly she was crying.

"That's right. Cry," Winifred said.

And behind them the will-less man, the failure.

Winifred cried out, "Go away, go away then," and Mrs. Baines slowly turned and came towards her husband.

"There, Mrs. B.," he said, "there then," and tended her his handkerchief.

Winifred bent low over the grave, and the fingers of one hand appeared to be tracing the anatomy of wreath and cross, then suddenly she leaned so far that I nearly cried out, "Careful, careful." It was as though she intended to lie there, craven under disaster.

"Oh, Tom!"

The two words seemed suspended in the air above her. Baines drew back until he was standing at my side, then he went forward a pace, until I was staring into the broad back.

"You see how it is, Charlie," he whispered.

I myself was stuttering in a moment. "I—I—I can hardly——"

"Sad, Charlie, sad, but it is a soul. It *is* a soul," he said.

"I understand."

"I am glad of that, Charlie," he replied, and then rejoined Mrs. Baines.

The shout from Winifred was probably expected by Mrs. Baines, and even by Baines himself, but not by me. Winifred was lying face downwards, her arms outstretched, embracing all, flower, and tomb, and cross. It seemed an age before anybody moved.

"On that bloody night," she cried.

Silence made an arch, nobody moved.

"I'm ready now," Winifred said, and so quietly into the morning air.

"Ready now, Charlie," Mr. Baines said, and I noticed his hand pressing upon Mrs. Baines's arm. I waited for them. Winifred left the grave. The Baineses drew back, and Winifred stepped into the path.

"Come along, Mrs. B.," and he led his wife away from the scene. I stood aside to let them pass. Suddenly Winifred stopped, half turned, leaned forward, as though some final urge in her would draw the sleeper from his bed. When Mr. Baines looked at me, I lowered my eyes. Winifred passed us, and after she had gone a little distance we followed behind her. A weird procession, and as before, in single file, as if within those gates none should dare to walk otherwise, after the wreath had been laid, after the gall had been spilled, after the duty had been done. Out of one path, and into another, then down the avenue of winter trees, and afar off, the first sight of the gates of iron. Baines doing his duty, gates opened, the party filing through, the gates closed.

"Out," I thought to myself. "*Out.*"

The formation held fast to the pavement, all the way to the bus stop. Winifred is always apart, withdrawn, locked within herself. Mr. and Mrs. Baines stand stiffly, closely, holding hands. I stood aloof, fascinated, confused, wondering. Baines spoke.

"Bus'll be here soon, Charlie."

"Thank you," and with great relief, I cried out, "So glad."

Winifred looked at me, Mrs. Baines, and finally Baines, but nothing was said. Then round the corner came the bus. We boarded it. There were three other passengers, sat close together for warmth on a rear seat. Our party ruthlessly split up, our seats became islands. The bus moved off to Lorne Road.

"When we get back," I thought, "we shall sit down together. What will be said? What will *I* say?"

"Keys Street," cried the conductor, and the trio in the back seat got out.

"Perhaps I'm dreaming."

"Perhaps it's all——" but Baines cut off any further speculation.

"Right, Charlie," he said.

"Here we are," announced Mrs. Baines.

And there we were, round the same corner, up the same street. Mr. Baines came up, took my arm.

"You see how it is, Charlie," he said.

"I do indeed."

I watched the quick movements of a curtain, met an eye, and thought to myself, "*Life* is somewhere about."

He pulled a key from his pocket, then ran on ahead of us. I kept the required distance behind the women.

"What an extraordinary journey."

We joined Baines at the door. The key turned in the lock.

"At last," I exclaimed under my breath. "At last."

Winifred was first in and made a dash to the parlour, banged the door in our faces.

"See to the oven, Mrs. B."

"I will see to everything, Mr. B."

Mrs. Baines vanished into the back kitchen. Baines remained standing in the hall.

"They're satisfied now," he said.

"Satisfied," I said, and my expression of utter bewilderment did not register.

We sat down.

"I'll go for a stroll, Mr. Baines."

"*Now?*"

"I think so."

"*Why?*"

"I want to. Why don't you come too."

"Me?"

The poker he held fell to the floor with a clatter.

"Some people likes going out, Charlie, and some doesn't."

"Don't you?"

"Not much really."

He picked up the poker, fidgeted with the coals.

"I noticed you don't have a radio set in the house, Mr. Baines."

"Sright," and suddenly, "Do we have to have one then, Charlie?"

I smiled. "Of *course* not, if you don't want to."

"You really are going out again?"

"Just for half an hour. *Do* come, Mr. Baines."

"Well, I don't know, Charlie, never was one for going out much, *really*."

"Just this once then?"

"Oh——" and he seemed to clutch more closely at the chair.

"*Do* come."

"Oh, all right then, Charlie, I will," he replied, yet made no effort to move.

"Come on, Mr. Baines."

"Very well," and he went straight to the door. "There, Mrs. B."

"Well then?"

"I'm going out," he said.

Mrs. Baines came into view at once. "What? On Sunday?"

"Sright. Shan't be long, just a short stroll with Charlie, then back again."

"You will be back then, Bainesy? S'unusual, isn't it, well, isn't it?"

"I said I won't be long, Mrs. B."

"*All* right," she said, and the weariness in her voice made me regret asking him. "I'll be upstairs," she said. "You know that."

"Oh, don't bother, really, Mr. Baines. It's not all that important. Forget it."

"S'orl right, Charlie. S'orl right. Said so."

He went off upstairs, and I waited for him in the hall. He returned wearing overcoat, scarf and the famous check cap.

"Stick then?" he asked.

"Stick?"

"It's here," he said, and handed me a walking-stick.

Mrs. Baines roared from within, "And don't you be too long, Mr. B."

"Very well."

Suddenly she was in the hall, watching us go.

"Very quiet around here," I said, as we stepped into the street.

"Sunday, Charlie. Always quiet here."

"I notice you don't have any newspapers in the house," I said.

"Sright. Used to one time. Not now. Rubbish, that's all. The lot."

We were half-way up the street when a door opened, and a man wearing a blue nap overcoat, white scarf and bowler emerged. He came slowly towards us. Suddenly he saw us, and stopped dead.

"Who's that, Mr. Baines?"

But Baines is stone deaf, increases his pace, and so do I.

The man drew nearer. I thought I heard a distant chortle.

"Seems to know you, Mr. Baines," I said.

And Baines is still deaf, still moving forward. The man stood waiting for us to pass.

"Is he?" I began, and suddenly Baines exclaimed under his breath, "Oh! Heavens above!"

When we reached him he gave Baines one look, and then exploded with laughter.

"Oh *God*, you Bainesy, *you*."

He rushed off, still laughing, and went on laughing until he turned the corner.

"*Who* on *earth* was that?" I asked.

"Chap name of Ted Spragge, Charlie, works up at Lawlers," and with great earnestness, "A scoffer, Charlie, that's all. Not to bother."

"Where shall we go, Mr. Baines?"

"Right to the top, then turn right," he said.

"Right," and we resumed our walk.

We stopped at the corner. "This way then?" I asked.

In a moment he was uncertain.

"Which *way*?"

And the Baines decision. "That way, Charlie."

Past the closed shops, the tightly shut doors, from area of silence to another.

"Down here?"

"Sright."

I stopped suddenly. "What is that?"

"Chapel."

"Oh."

"Call it The Rise, Charlie."

45

"*Do* they."

A very redoubtable-looking erection, a rocky bastion in Garlston.

"Turn here," he said. "Old brick works at the end of this road, Charlie. Used to walk there from The Rise some Sunday mornings, used to sit in a bit of clearing down there. Overgrown now, of course. Lots of things overgrown to-day, Charlie."

"When was that, Mr. Baines?"

"Time ago now. Bit younger then."

"Down *here*?"

"Sright," he said, and we were soon stumbling over the loose stones.

"Careful there."

"Listening to Winifred this morning, Mr. Baines, it struck me that——" And then I closed like a clam, and when I opened my mouth again it was to stutter at Baines, "No, no, it didn't, it's all right, Mr. Baines. *Here?*"

Baines nodded, and he gave me a queer look.

"Bench down at the end here, Charlie. Often used to sit there in the old days."

And on we clambered over the stones. Once or twice I slipped.

"Careful, Charlie, *careful*, not so headlong, where's it get you then?"

Our feet made loud crunching noises as we toiled on, and toiled seemed the appropriate description.

"Terribly overgrown, Mr. Baines. And rather hideous, if I may say so, I mean the whole thing," and at once my arms were waving in all directions. "Well, look at it! The *lot*."

"Nobody notices much now, Charlie, not to-day, no *time*, that's how everything is. Sit here. There! Wait. Just a minute. There now! Hanky where you sit. Sright."

"Phew! What a climb," I said.

"'Tis a bit then."

Baines draped the bench with his bulk, and I sat down beside him.

"Mind?"

"Not at all."

He fingered his pipe, and I lit a cigarette.

"You all strike me as being very fond of the house," I said.

"Theirs. *Told* you."

He puffed vigorously at the pipe, sent clouds over Garlston.

"I had heard."

Baines was alert. "Had you then. From Mrs. B. then?"

"Does Winifred go out at all?"

"Not over much, sometimes Sundays, and sometimes *she* thinks as how she might go out sometime, and mayn't get back at all."

"How odd."

The bench creaks, and Joshua looks thoughtful.

"Have you been married long, Mr. Baines?"

"*She* married me, Charlie."

"I see. If you *hadn't* married Mrs. Baines?"

"Still be at Lawlers working, just the same. If Mrs. B. went out, Charlie, and Winifred's there when she gets back, she looks jealous at once like she'd stand no nonsense anyhow. I *like* our Winifred being around, cause I'm close enough any-time to Mrs. Baines."

"Does Mrs. Baines work, too?"

"Sright. At Lawlers."

"What does Mrs. Baines do? Hammer in the nails like you?"

"Not nails, Charlie, no. Odd jobber and such. Sticks on labels, wraps up, checks in-goings, out-goings, makes tea for Mr. Crawley, helps generally, Charlie, if you know what I mean."

"I think I do."

"Never late once, Charlie, off together, back together, that's how it is."

"Did you ever want to do anything else? I mean apart from working at Lawlers?"

"Not really. All our lot were nails, Charlie, my father, *his*, they was half-timers, sort of grew up in it, you might say, then Dad was drawn in——"

"*Drawn* in?"

"Sright. Into a mach*ine*, Charlie. No good when they drew him out, no. Was me hurrying from school there that day, to Lawlers I mean, ah—saw the last of school that day, ah——" and Baines sighed, and remembered. "Glad, Charlie, *glad*. Didn't like much that Mr. Poole. S'bugger for you, if you'll excuse me, hated him, I did, *really*, laughed too often, did Poole, I thought, even then——"

"Laughed. At what?"

"*Me*. Always laughing at me, first name I ever had at school was wooden head, come out of his mouth often, even that morning Dad was drawn in, Charlie, even *then*. 'God Almighty, Baines,' he said, 'and what am I going to do with you, you've failed *again*.' He threw my exam papers all over the room that morning. 'Who keeps putting sawdust into your head, Baines,' he said. Course I never answered him, just run straight off to Lawlers where they'd just got him *out* when I got there."

Baines paused for a moment, then continued.

"When Dad died, Charlie, only friend I had left was Christ. Mean that, fact. All right then, I said to myself that awful morning, all right, you'll keep to yourself now, Baines, and I did. That time Mother give me the Book, first time I'd heard about it, and she said to me, 'Joshua, in this Book you will find one that will not laugh at you.' And I did. So I kept it ever since. I *told* you, Charlie, I live by the Word now. *I* know what I've got inside me, and it's much less than what I haven't. I'm what you'd call a quiet liver, and I'm nothing much, and I couldn't never get away from nails now, Charlie, never. Full life maybe, maybe not, all account of how you look at it. Sright."

There was something sad about Baines, and in some curious sense, something beautiful, sitting there on an old bench, under glowering clouds, up on this rise from the town, the tight town, and the tighter house. What a big man he is, and the vastness of frame fascinates me. He hadn't wanted to leave the house at all, but suddenly I realized he was only too anxious to get back again.

"Ever wish to be anything else, Mr. Baines? For instance, when you were a boy at school?"

He shook his head, and there was something inevitable, terribly final for Baines.

"You just knew what you had to be, Charlie. Nobody asked me what I wanted to do, s'no use, s'fixed, *they* knew already, *then*, fixed, fixed. They *all* knew. The others, I mean. Had to *be*, where I lived, where they lived. No dodging allowed in Garlston, Charlie."

"I understand that well enough," I said.

"I'm glad of that," he said.

"Who taught you the flute?"

"Dad."

"Do you play much?"

"Not now, Charlie," he said, intensely confiding, like the closing of arms, "not now, count of Mrs. B. not liking music much. Sometimes I do play, but I sit *out* of the house, Charlie, in my shed, play low there sometimes."

"If I may ask, Mr. Baines. How old is Winifred?"

"Makes no odds either way, *now*. Not now, Charlie. Too late. Look at her then, half mad, ah—*she* wanted Tom, wanted their lives together, for always. Remember the first evening I ever met him, laughed his head off at something I said. Endo for Winifred, Charlie, when he finally kipped, fact. Broke her up. S'fact."

"I expect she'll meet somebody one day and be happy again."

"Too late. What you don't know, Charlie, is our Winifred. Only wanted Tom."

"Want a light? Your pipe's gone out."

"Love's love to Winifred, real, *binds*. One man, Charlie, one, s'real as that then, *real*."

"Would you have liked children, Mr. Baines?"

"Too late."

He paused, and added slowly, "S'pipe dream, and now I'm locked up."

And then a very pronounced ahem. His pipe had gone out.

"*She* took him, Charlie, what never wanted kids anyhow, for Mrs. Baines any kid kicks the pence out of the way, and she likes the pence. Told you.

"Should've seen her that night, catching them at it, Mrs. B. and Tom, terrible, awful, shock on her hope, Charlie. Mrs. Carles was shocked, too, nearly swallowed the needles she had in her teeth. Never come any more to the house after that."

"Your pipe's gone out. Want a light?"

"Ta."

"Mrs. Baines seems to be very fond of money," I said.

"You said that anywhere in Lawler neighbourhood, Charlie, they'd know where *you* come from."

"Where?"

"Down there of course," and he suddenly laughed.

It was the first time I had heard him laugh, a single "ha".

"Give all my money up to Mrs. B. 'cept a few bob that I don't do much with anyhow, I mean count of what Mrs. B. knows, Charlie, what her dad knew, what *I* knew. You save in case of the fall. If Mrs. B. lost a penny she'd shudder. Fact. From the time you open your eyes in this world, Charlie, you pray you won't fall count of that, I mean no job, sudden, like *that*," and he flicked finger and thumb. "Fall low indeed if you haven't saved. *I* know."

"Of course you do, Mr. Baines."

For a big man he rose very quickly. "Going now, Charlie, must go."

"But we've only just come out," I said, "surely—another quarter of an hour, I'm enjoying talking to you."

"*Are* you, Charlie?"

"Think I'll stay a little longer," I said. "I might walk up *that* way."

"You'll do what you want to do," he said. "Most people does, I *hope*."

I got up. We faced each other, and he put his hands on my shoulders.

"Won't say nothing to anybody, Charlie, about what I said to you this minute. Honest?"

He looked me straight in the eye.

"Of course not, why should I?"

He stared hard at me, seeming a little uncertain, the committed man.

"Let's go then, Charlie."

But something wasn't quite finished, for suddenly he was seated again. The bench groaned.

"Was it always like this?" I asked.

"Used to be just grass one time, walked off by feet long ago, Charlie, so *many* feet now."

"Tell me, Mr. Baines, and I hope you don't mind my asking this, but do you ever feel sorry for Mrs. Baines?"

"Not for her sin, Charlie," he said.

"Her sin?"

"Stealing another's life, Charlie. If everybody forgive everybody for their sins you couldn't begin to reckon up as on what would happen."

"You don't mean that this will go on and on?"

"What goes on and on then?" and his tone was sharp, almost accusing.

"Well, this visit to Garlan Road," I said.

"Life goes on and on, Charlie, well, doesn't it then?"

"And nobody *minds*?"

"A thing's easier when you don't mind," he said, paused for a moment, and added with great seriousness, "Sometimes you don't mind, Charlie, and sometimes you *daren't*."

"Good God."

"What's that then?"

"Nothing, nothing."

I could feel his breath against my ear.

"I am glad of that, Charlie," he said, with great relief.

His head fell forward a little, and the two hands knotted themselves on the ample knees. A silence fell between us. I thought of Baines concentrating on the thing to be done, the ritualistic walk back to Baptist Street.

"What does Mrs. Baines do?"

"Works, Charlie, *works*."

"That all?"

"Sright."

I turned abruptly. "Let's go," I said.

It seemed suddenly wrong for Baines to be here at all, islanded in this peaceful backwater, amidst the desert of bricks and stones, and the stumps of blackened trees, under a sky of heavy, low-lying clouds. So this was where he came to sit in the old days, probably alone, probably wanting to be, that kind of person, for whom life was perhaps the nightmare of the hurrying feet, the town heavy with them, as he explained to me so forcibly, and the distance from the bench and the nails ever the same. Perhaps remembering the days of his father, and Mr. Poole, and the sawdust in his head, the thought of the "fall" always uppermost, long before the dream in the dark corner, that breaking of chains, that running away. And coming early to the Book, its pages living in his hand.

He took out an enormous silver watch attached to a heavy chain.

"S'time, Charlie," he said, his voice now gentle, like father, and uncle, and friend, "s'time, Charlie."

"I'm sure it is," I replied, resigned now to his restlessness, to his wish to be off.

We left the bench far behind us, and I watched his bulk move slowly, tormentingly, over the uneven ground. We stood together for a moment, looked away towards the town.

"Did you used to go to The Rise?"

"Sright. Dad and Mother, aunts, the lot. Gone now. Ah well."

"Let's get on," I said.

Again the caution, the care.

"Careful again, Charlie, then careful, lad."

"Do you like your work, Mr. Baines?"

"No use not liking what you have to do, is there then?"

"I suppose not."

The Baines interest in the Baineses is something that has to be experienced. It has certainly engendered a modesty in myself.

"Do *you* ever go to the sea, Mr. Baines?"

"Went to Lytham once. Time ago, can't remember, really, doesn't matter much, careful then, Charlie, *care*ful."

The level ground at last, the crunching of gravel.

"Very few people about," I remarked.

"Sunday, Charlie."

The Rise came into view. "An odd name," I said.

"Not really. Place where God rises, and men rise, I *hope*."

"We all hope."

He made no reply, and perhaps didn't wish to be bothered. We paused to look at the chapel. The closed door needed a coat of paint, the calls to prayer and salvation, in the brightest colours, now hung forlornly from their black boards.

"Is it ever open these days?"

"Sometimes, Charlie. Sometimes, always Sunday evenings, yes. People's moody about the Book these days. Expect you know that."

I nodded. "Very few young people about."

A stout finger pointed over the town. "Down there always, Sundays," he said. "Always find them down there, any place that is lit up, Charlie, and not always with lights neither."

We turned the corner, and there was Baptist Street. As we walked down I kept my eyes fixed on the windows. In this long street they remain my sole fascination. What kind of life is locked behind those curtains, those shut doors?

"Here we are, Charlie. Home."

I became aware of a frantically waving hand, and then I saw Winifred sitting in the window. She was smiling, and yet there was something frantic in her look. Baines pushed his key in the door.

"*In*, Charlie, in."

I was gently propelled down the green corridor. The door closed.

"There," he exclaimed, and *what* a sigh of relief. "Just going upstairs now, Charlie, you sit to the fire, Charlie. Enjoy the stroll?"

"Very much indeed."

"Glad of that."

Poor Baines seems almost glad of anything. I heard him call.

"You there, Mrs. Baines?"

"Here, Mr. B. Where I always am."

"Well then, I'm back now."

"Where's *he*?"

"Charlie's down here then."

54

"She huggin' herself in the parlour's usual?"

"You know where she is, Mrs. B., you *know*, why *ask*?"

"Call her then."

"Winifred!—*Wini*—fred."

The kitchen door burst open, and there was Winifred.

"Back then?"

"Yes," I said.

The door slammed hard. No door in this house closes quietly. I imagine a special hatred spinning between Winifred's fingers.

"Where'd *he* go then?"

"We went for a walk as far as the old quarry," I said.

"*He* say anything?"

"I don't quite understand, Winifred."

"No—you wouldn't then."

Baines plodded slowly upstairs.

"That you?"

"It is."

"Ready now," Winifred said, rushed into the hall, and shouted, "Are *you* coming then?"

She sat down, waited for *him*.

"She rests, Sundays, Charlie."

"Who?"

"Mrs. B."

"Oh! I see. And Mr. Baines?"

"He rests. Went out with you then, did he say anything about me?"

"Nothing at all."

She had folded her arms on the table, and now she leaned over and spoke slowly, in a low voice. "Sure then?"

"Of course."

The shout shook the house. "Are you *coming*?"

The answer came in heavy treads downstairs. Baines came in.

"Sright now," he said, and sat down.

"Isn't Mrs. Baines coming down?" I asked.

"Mrs. Baines never has dinner Sunday, Charlie, just rests."

"Oh!" and I couldn't have said more.

Winifred served us. I fully expected Baines to reach out for the Book, but he ignored it, concentrated upon his dinner, and I did likewise. Winifred's plate was the lightest of all. We ate in silence.

"Charlie liked the country," Baines said.

"Did he then?" a grudge, almost a snarl in the voice.

"Did you like the country, Charlie?"

"It was very nice."

"There, our Winifred. Didn't I *tell* you he liked it," Baines said.

"More, Charlie?"

"Just a little," I said.

"Eat up, Charlie," said Mr. Baines, "do *eat*," and I did my best.

3

Winifred looked me straight in the eye. "I like the sea best."

"*Do* you?"

"Love the sea, Charlie."

Suddenly I knew what was strange. No words from the Book, no bells.

"Eat up," Mr. Baines said.

"Yes, eat up then," said Winifred.

"Like it?"

"Very nice," I said, though I must confess that I hardly noticed *what* I was eating. I felt as if I had drawn back with me a long hallucinatory thread from tomb to table. Not a sound from above. Perhaps the hour of meditation. Baines wiped his mouth, got up, pushed in his chair. He looked seriously at us both, and then went out.

"Mr. Baines always rests Sundays, Charlie."

"Does he?"

I listened to the squeak of the Baines boots, the heavy tread on uncarpeted stairs.

"I said Mr. Baines always rests Sundays."

I sat up, dropped my spoon. "Rests?" I paused a moment. "*Rests?*"

"More pie?"

"Thanks, I will."

"It is hard work at Lawlers."

"I'm sure it is."

Astounding, Winifred has actually talked to me, told me something, as if she *wants* to, and she loves the sea.

"Fancy your liking the sea. I'm very fond of it myself."

"Are you then? 'Swonderful to me, Charlie."

A winter sun shines through the window, and the water dances in my glass. I wait for any further crumb that may fall.

"Do you ever go to the sea?"

"Not now," rather sadly, I thought.

"What a pity."

She made no reply, but stared out through the window. Winifred has the greyest eyes, and her thick black hair is pulled rudely back from the forehead. She has a thin mouth. I could not guess her age. The lips are slightly parted, seem always so, as though within the words lie waiting.

"What do you do on Sundays, Winifred?"

"Nothing."

"*Nothing?*"

"And Mr. Baines rests. And your sister?"

"She rests."

"Mrs. Baines works at Lawlers."

"Sright, Charlie. That's where she met Bainesy. Show you them on their wedding *day*," suddenly got up and went to the door. "*Show* you."

And there she was, waiting. I followed her out, entered the front room.

"There they are," and she pointed to the mantelpiece, "s'nice, isn't it?"

"Very nice," and I stood staring down at the formidable Mrs. Baines, so very close to the man of nails.

"He's soft, Charlie," she said, drew close, leaned her elbow on the mantelpiece, gave me a shy smile.

I had the back view of those stiff white curtains. There was a large plant pressing its foliage against the glass. And everywhere, photographs, in heavy oak frames. Various branches of the Baines family stared back at me. A huge, round mahogany table almost filled the room, upon which stood another plant, the leaves of which seemed to be pushing their way towards the ceiling. Against the wall, a couch, and on the end of it, neatly piled bedclothes. Her bed, obviously.

"This is *your* room?"

"Sright. I often sit in the window there, Sundays," she said. "Like to see the people going past, especially some Sundays. *Once*, Charlie, I actually thought I *saw* Tom walking up the street," and after a slight pause, a sudden burst, "It was lovely, Charlie, *lovely*—he used to——" and then her voice faltered.

It was the moment of embarrassment.

"I'm sure it was, Winifred. Now, I think I'll go upstairs to my room."

"Do what you want to do," she replied, stiffly, harshly.

Yet I made no move, but remained close to her. There seems room for two Winifreds inside her black dress, an enveloping garment that imprisoned from toes to head. One hand gripped the mantelpiece.

"Does Mr. Baines go out *very* much?" I asked.

"He had such nice eyes, Charlie, and hair very fair, very."

"It's cold in here," I said, "let's go back to the kitchen."

"She's going to tell me about Tom," I thought.

I sat in the Baines corner, and she sat in the other.

"Sometimes we used to go to the football, Saturdays. I liked that."

"*Did* you?"

"Such a splendid man, Charlie."

"I'm sure he was. I'm very sorry, very sorry indeed."

"*Are* you?" doubting it.

"Of *course*. This is a very quiet street, Winifred."

"Very quiet, Charlie, always is, *really*, hear that," and she sat bolt upright.

"Hear what?"

"S'only them next door. Cis Foulkes and her lot. They go out a lot, Charlie, but nobody knows *where*."

"Foulkes?"

"Sright. Noisy lot."

"Are they?"

"Born where the world's noise is, Charlie, that's what."

"Mind if I smoke?"

"Do what you want to do. Die in this street, Charlie, and nobody'd *ever* know."

I lit a cigarette. "Does it matter?"

And then an explosion. "No."

She leaned towards me, kneaded her fingers, watched me.

"He was the cleanest man I ever knew, Charlie, always a collar to him, and Saturdays washed all over, never failed. He *was* a clean man."

"Who?" I said, forgetting.

"Tom," she said, "who else then?"

What does Winifred see out of the front-room window? How far does she look?

"Don't you ever have a fire in your room, Winifred?"

"Sometimes Sundays, but mostly in here, sit here when they go up. Mrs. B. vowed she'd never let this fire go out after Dad died."

"Why?"

"Ask her."

"Does she go out much?"

"Her? If she goes anywhere, he'd go, too. He's like that, Charlie, soft."

"But surely," I said, "you don't all sit in the house like this. Does nobody go out then?"

"When we have to, Charlie. Like a nice cup of tea then?"

"I don't think so, really. I'm going up to my room now, there are matters needing my attention."

And the childish response. "Have you, Charlie?"

She leaned forward again, her hands pressed flat upon her knees. They were good hands, well shaped, but coarsened, reddened by hard work. One felt that the long, slender fingers should have been whiter.

"First time Tom *saw* Bainesy he laughed, Charlie, laughed out loud, couldn't help it, couldn't stop sort of—'Look at his head, Winnie,' he said, 'might be filled with boiled taters.'"

She laughed. "It was funny."

"I expect you've friends calling from time to time."

Her eyes widened, she leaned even closer, and asked, "Who then?"

And for the moment I just hadn't the answer.

"Oh, I don't know—well—Tom, Dick and Harry perhaps."

"Never knew they were friends of Bainesy, or her, besides which he couldn't have any, and she wouldn't."

"Wouldn't what?"

"Wouldn't have friends, Charlie. They don't mind."

"Good Lord."

"Half a minute," she cried, jumped to her feet, and ran out of the kitchen.

Nobody calls. Nobody minds. She doesn't, and he wouldn't. Winifred's replies echo in my ear. But why don't they have friends? Don't they *want* any? Why do they remain in the house? I seemed to be seeing this kitchen as for the first time, with its everlasting fire, and the great ugly fireplace, and uglier armchairs, the big oak dresser that was topped by a fierce wooden eagle, the cluster of loud vases containing ferns, the table, and its too-bright cloth, the big teapot on the hob that made one think in sculptural terms, and as in the front room, the mantelpiece loaded with photographs. There was the sound of crockery being washed.

"I can't sit here all day talking to her," I told myself, and as I rose Winifred came in, sat down, and said, "Do sit, Charlie. So restless."

"Do you work at Lawlers?"

"Work here, Charlie."

"When did you last go to the sea?"

"Long time ago."

"How often do *you* go out?"

"Not much. Not now. Don't mind, really. I'll just be here, Charlie, close. Be close to her forever, she *knows* that," and suddenly, and surprisingly vicious, "I'll be there when she sinks. Close to her, very close."

"Is this Mr. Baines's house?"

"Ours."

"Oh," and it was all I could say, in the absence of anything else.

"When Tom was here I used to go out sometimes *then*. He liked going out; we once went to Barnton, Charlie, 'slovely at Barnton, crowds of course, didn't like them much, no, but lovely all the same; first time I'd ever seen the donkeys there; 'sfunny, all at once I felt I'd like to be a donkey girl, just loved them little things, and what d'you think, straightaway I went up to the man as owns them, asked him, said I'd like to be a donkey girl at Barnton; course he only laughed, never heard anything like that, he hadn't, 'sfunny to him, I mean a girl wanting to look after donkeys. Even Tom laughed, so when he did, I had to, of course, that *time*. 'Be just a nice girl, Winnie,' Tom said. That's what my mother used to say to me, Charlie, be a nice girl. One day the insurance man called and I was playing on the step, and he said to me hand under my chin, 'And what are you going to be when you grow up, little girl,' and mother said, 'She'll be a nice girl, won't you, dear,' and I said nothing because I didn't know, *really*; bit of a kid then, so I suppose that's it."

62

The words cascaded out.

"Tell me, Winifred, were you ever——"

"Had *his* trousers off only three months after Tom died. She's like that, Charlie, can't never get enough *enough*, and then *he* came here, big fat slob is Bainesy, and talking out of him ever since in this house as if God Almighty was his uncle, course she's *like* that, Charlie, Mrs. Baines, I mean, my sister, I *told* you, *and* she loves money, loves having it, and having more of it all the time, save save *save*, that's her, to an end nobody knows about, or what for, or why. *She* never minded what any man's head's full of, Charlie. Never will, I reckon, but *I'll* be there all the time, *all* the time, never leave her side now, never. . . ."

I leaned forward myself. "What I meant to say——"

"Wouldn't miss nothing she wouldn't, never has, never will, hates losing anything, Charlie, *anything*. She's like that, she daren't lose a farthing, a chance, a halfpenny, a crumb, an inch, a penny stamp, a second, *nothing*, moving on it all the time, all the time, money, money, money, just loves it——"

"*Do* tell me, Winifred——"

"Night Tom lay down for good I thought I'd die, Charlie, oh *Christ*, I rushed out, I had to, out of this *bloody* house—I—I——"

She burst into tears, and at the same time there came a roar from above.

"Winifred—*Wini*-fred——"

"Please. Don't cry," I said, and almost without realizing it I found my hand in her own. "Please."

"Had to go out that time, had to, Charlie. Didn't care much, didn't care how, went up all streets come down again, then I was running anywhere, everywhere. God, I cried that time, Charlie, cried."

Her bitter sobs appeared to be unheard by Baines.

"I'm so sorry," I said. "I expect you'll meet some nice man and get married—I——"

"Nothing's good twice, Charlie, you know that," and she dropped my hand like a stone.

"Have you always lived here, Winifred?"

"Always, where else can you live then, where else?"

"Were you born here?"

"I was. Worse luck. Notice Mr. B. Nails on the brain, Charlie, that's what this place is."

"Mr. Baines was saying that he and his wife both go off together, and return together. Is it always like that?"

She turned away for a moment to wipe her eyes, suddenly spluttered into her handkerchief.

"She'll never let him out of her sight now, and he doesn't mind."

"Mr. Baines doesn't appear to mind anything, Winifred."

"A thing's easier when you don't mind, that's what he said. Always says it, doesn't care either way, *really*."

"What do you do in the evenings?" I asked.

She seemed more composed, her voice calmer. She put away the handkerchief.

"I go to my room, Charlie, and they go upstairs."

"Every evening?"

"Sright. Sometimes we sit in here by the fire, Charlie."

"And then what?"

"He talks to her about his life, and she talks to him about hers."

"Is *that* all?"

"Sometimes he reads to her from the Book, Charlie."

"How extraordinary. And you? You just listen, and if you don't want to, you go to your room. Is that it?"

"Sright, Charlie."

"But surely, Winifred, I mean—well, don't you want to do *anything*? What about outside? The world?"

"What about it?"

"*Well*, other *people*, living in the world. Friends—are there no relations at all? It's—I mean I—*really*——"

"Bainesy only goes out at all because he has to, the nails I mean, so does she, but he don't much like the world anyhow. Sometimes he says to me, I mean when that *bitch* is really out of his sight, he says, 'D'you know what I want to do *really*, Winifred, do you then,' and I said, 'What's that, Mr. B.,' and he said, 'I want to walk as far away from myself as I can,' *far* away, he said, and the *way* he said it, Charlie, believing in that so *much*, *wanting* to, course I said to him, 'Why then,' and he said, 'Because I'm nothing, because I *know* I'm nothing,' and he only wants to run *off*. Gets him bad, Charlie, real bad, only one thing in his head now, s'fact."

"Yes. What's that?"

"God Almighty," she said, "and if you left him out, then what's left then, what?"

"What *is*?"

"Nothing. Empty, Charlie. He cries sometimes, just thinking about it, I mean him being nothing much."

"He did mention to me some humiliation at school, Winifred, some man by the name of Poole. He seems never to have forgotten it."

"When you haven't much inside, Charlie, you put your claws on what you have, hang on, s'fact, have to. Mrs. B. once said to him, 'Bainesy, you'll have to live a whole bloody life being nothing'——"

"What a dreadful thing to say to him, Winifred."

"She's *like* that, Charlie, told you. Bitch from the heels up, s'fact."

"Poor Mr. Baines," I said.

"Did *he* tell you that then, about old Pooley, ah, if only he *could* do that then, if only, I'd be glad, know why then?"

"Why?"

"Because Mr. B.'d be happy, Charlie."

"But if Mr. Baines went away, Winifred, you'd be left with her," I said.

"Oh God! I never thought of that, Charlie," she said, and round-eyed, she stared at me.

"But if you went, too," I said, "she'd be left alone, why don't *you* go away?"

"Can't now."

"But why?"

"Daren't."

"What *would* make you happy?" I asked.

She flung herself forward, and exclaimed, "Oh, Charlie, if he—if only," and I knew.

If Tom is not clawing at Winifred, she is clawing at Tom. She gripped my hand, held fast, and said slowly, "If Tom rose up out of that bloody grave——"

"Don't cry."

"I'm not crying."

"You *are*."

And she was, suddenly slumped across the table.

I wanted to go, and I hated going. Suddenly Baines was calling again, "Winifred!"

And a moment later, "Wini—*fred*!"

"Mr. Baines is calling."

"*Let* him."

"Can I do anything?" and wondered what it would be.

She was erect in a moment. "Leave me *alone*."

And I decided to leave her alone. I got up and went to the door, but she was behind me, pulling on my arm.

"Charlie?"

"Well?"

And almost in desperation, "Don't go," and lowering her voice, she added, "Don't say nothing, will you, Charlie?"

"I won't," I said.

"To them upstairs."

"I *said* I won't."

"*Char*lie?"

"Well?"

"She says I'm mad, she tells him that, and he never minds at all."

"Do they stay upstairs the whole afternoon?"

"Sright."

"You have all your meals in your own room?"

"'Cept Sundays that is, have dinner with Bainesy then."

"What do they do up there on Sundays?"

"Never asked, never looked, Charlie, just lie there, I suppose."

"Do you always sit in the window on Sundays?"

"Sright."

"Do tell me, what is it you see out of the window?"

"What I want to see."

"Sometimes we can't help seeing what we don't *want* to see," I said.

The air in this house is yesterday's, and the day before that.

"D'you never open a window in this house, Winifred?" I asked.

The question surprised her.

"We open them, Charlie, but we always shut them again."

"I can't open mine. I've tried."

"Give it a real good push then."

"I did."

"Tell her. She'll do it in a tick, Charlie."

"I'm sure she would. I must ask her this evening."

"Sright."

"Don't you ever feel the cold?"

"Sometimes. Don't really feel the cold, Charlie."

This kitchen holds the heat of hell, but the hall is always cold. I thought of the front door. "How strange," I thought, "nobody ever knocks at this house," and I wondered why.

"What are you staring at, Charlie?" she asked.

"Nothing," I said, "I was just thinking."

67

"Oh!"

"I'm going up to my room now, Winifred. What will you do?"

"I'll be in mine till teatime, Charlie."

I got up, and I was glad to get up. "And then?" I said.

"If she comes down with him, *and* she might, I'll stay where I am."

"I see," though I wasn't quite certain, even about that.

"He'll be out there, Charlie," and suddenly she too got up, pointing to the window. "Out there."

I followed her to the window. I looked out on a paved back yard, at the foot of which there stood a painted wooden shed.

"There!" she said and continued pointing. "Two nights a week he goes out, glad to sometimes, hiding away from her, don't know what Bainesy'd do if he didn't have his old flute."

"I heard about that," I said.

She swung round. "Seems to have been talking his head off to you, Charlie, s'funny that, usually it's just, 'Yes, Mrs. B., no, Mrs. B.,' with him. Her man and dog that's what he is, way he goes on, used to make Tom ache when he was here——"

"They were both here then, Winifred?"

"Till he died and she didn't give a damn, she didn't. God! You should have seen me that night, Charlie, I—longed for him, told you, went everywhere he'd used to walk, longed for him, even out of the stones I did. Night's the worst, the worst, darkness wrapping you up, dropping you down, leaving you alone, Charlie, *alone*. Nothing's like him, nothing."

After the outburst, the silence seemed intense.

"What a shame."

"Have to talk to somebody sometimes, Charlie. If Tom'd lived, if he hadn't bumped into her, I'd be——" and then words failed her, and she returned to her seat by the fire. "I can't

68

help it," she said, "I just can't. I hate the living sight of her now."

I returned to my seat, sat down. "Winifred," I said.

She sat up. "Well then?"

"You can't go on like this, surely, there must be an end to it."

"I'll wear her out, Charlie, that's what I'll do."

"You all seem afraid of one another. I mean you——"

"Well?"

She jumped to her feet. "I'm going to my room now, Charlie," she said, and went.

When I heard the heavy footsteps on the stairs I realized why.

"What extraordinary people," I thought, and then Baines himself came in.

"There you are, Charlie."

"Here I am."

"Heard you talking to her," he said and took the vacant armchair.

"Yes. We were chatting," I said.

"Mrs. B.'s on her way down now, Charlie."

"Is she?"

"Sright. You won't be minding then," and out came the pipe.

"Not at all."

The Baines hair is tousled, the eyes seem only half open. Looking at him as he leaned towards me, I thought, "This afternoon Baines smells stale. Perhaps he sleeps in his clothes."

"Tea, Winifred, tea then!" he roared.

"I thought Winifred took all her meals in her own room, Mr. Baines."

He replied casually, "Sometimes she does, sometimes she doesn't."

He called again. "*Wini*fred!"

"I'm not deaf!" shouted Winifred.

Baines gave a sudden yawn, then slowly turned his bulk towards the fire.

"Been studying in your room then, Charlie?"

"No, I wasn't. The fire looked cosy enough, I stayed down."

"Oh!"

"It still seems odd to me, Mr. Baines, that you don't have a radio, or even a newspaper in the house."

"In this house, Charlie, we just do what we want to do, and that's all."

The door opened again, Mrs. Baines came in.

"There you are, Mrs. B. Sit then," Joshua said, and she sat.

"I could hear you talking down here, Charlie, to our Winifred."

"Yes, that's right. We had a chat," I said.

She turned accusing eyes on me, and asked, "What about then?"

"Tittle tattle, really," I said.

Suddenly Baines sat erect, knocked out his pipe, and exclaimed abruptly, "Charlie's sad, Mrs. B."

"Are you sad, Charlie?" she asked. "Some people are, of course. I hear our Winifred talking down here, wondered what nonsense rattled out of her head."

"Ssh!" Mr. Baines said.

"You were talking a *long* time, Charlie," Mrs. Baines said.

"That's right. I said so, Mrs. Baines."

"Charlie's sad because we haven't no radio, Mrs. B., and no newspapers neither. Where he comes from they have to lean on so many things, that's right, Charlie, isn't it then?"

I smiled, I had to.

"I'm not sad at all, Mrs. Baines. But it did seem strange to me, as I remarked to Mr. Baines. He hasn't even heard of the bomb——"

"Oh yes," she said, and concentrated her attention on me. "Well then?"

"Well, there's only one," I said, "and everybody's talking about it, dreaming about it, and they can't make up their minds about it, one way or the other. Some want it clean, some want it dirty. Some *like* talking about it, some like *liking* it, Mrs. Baines, so that they can go on talking about it. That's all I talked about to Mr. Baines."

When she leaned across the table, I drew back. Mrs. Baines is at any time formidable.

"What about it then?"

I looked at Baines. He looked at me out of puppy blue eyes, and appeared quite unruffled.

"I told Charlie, Mrs. B., that there was only one bomb worth talking *about*."

"Quite right, Mr. B. Is *she* coming or *isn't* she then?"

The bull neck strained, and Baines cried, "Our *Wini*fred."

The tea came in on a tray. Winifred put it on the table and sat down.

"Last night, Charlie," and in a moment Baines was like father, like son and brother, "last night I showed you the lot, well, didn't I? Didn't throw up that window for nothing. You *saw* them. Well then, didn't you *see* them, Charlie?"

"Excuse me," I said, and turned to Winifred. "Winifred, why don't you have this chair? Much more comfortable."

Her head remained bent, she did not raise it.

"I'll sit where I want to sit. Will somebody give me my *cup*."

"Here then," Joshua said.

"What Mr. B. means, Charlie," said Mrs. Baines, "what he means is this, they can't never have enough, have to have the things, can't not stop wanting everything, have to go, can't not stop going to them places, doing them things, everything at their *hand*, Charlie."

"Like Aladdin's lamp, Charlie, *everything*. They call it having what's what in the world to-day, don't they, Mrs. B.?"

"Sright."

"Is a chap alongside me on my bench, Charlie, at Lawlers, come up to me and said, 'Baines, I wish to God I could get excited about *something*, but I *can't*.' Think of that, Charlie, and he has the lot."

"The lot?"

"Sright. What you all got to-day, too many things to lean on, can't stand upright less you have them, never will *now*. Too late."

Mrs. Baines's cup remained suspended in the air.

"What Mr. B. means," she said, then paused, "what he means, Charlie, is this," and she paused again, looked at Joshua. "What was his name, Mr. B.? That chap, oh, you know then——"

"Engleworth, Jack Engleworth. Married. Two kids. Lives up Daisy Lane, have everything, worried in case they won't, daren't not think about not having them, I *told* you, Charlie."

"*Told* me?"

"Have everything, Charlie, without as much as moving their arses, everything, Engleworth's lot, telly, radio, two gramophones, ale in the telly cabinet, a washing machine, hair dryer for her. *She* has Government teeth, him specks. Daughter Sandra's married twice, nineteen she is, lives on top of her parents with two bastards, Government allowance for each. Lucky she's only one daughter, lucky for some man later turning a corner meeting her, like it happens sometimes, call it fate. That's what Mr. B. *means*, Charlie. Have to lean on everything now, no bone, now they want the moon. S'pity so much of it's called sense, you know by *who*——"

"Who, Mrs. Baines?"

"Tell him, Mr. Baines."

"I'll tell him time enough, Mrs. B. And now I'm going out."

"You like music, Charlie?" asked Mrs. Baines.

"Yes, I do. I said so."

"Course you did. Well then, Bainesy's going out to his little den, said he'd play the flute for you if you like that——"

Winifred jumped to her feet, and rushed from the kitchen. The door banged. Baines remained poised over the table.

Mrs. Baines looked up. "Are you going then, Mr. B.? Or aren't you?"

"I'm going," he said.

"She's got a wound in her belly, Charlie, hates being alone with me any time, doesn't she, Bainesy?"

"Leave her alone, Mrs. B. Coming, Charlie?"

In this house one has no sooner got up from the table than one is sitting down again. It has occurred to me that the Baines family is fond of eating and drinking. I got up, pushed in the chair.

"Of course," I said, and I was glad to.

Mrs. Baines stared into the fire, addressed her husband over her shoulder. "I'll call you when it's time. Go on, Charlie," she urged, "see his little den. He simply loves it."

I left her relaxed, comfortable in the matriarchal chair. I would have given many pennies for her thoughts. I went through the back kitchen where I found Baines standing over the sink, looking out of the window. I wondered what *he* saw. He didn't move as I came up behind him.

"S'getting dark now, Charlie," he said.

"So it is."

"This way then."

We walked out into the yard. I stopped half-way, looked back at the house, the closed door.

"It is shut, Charlie, 'sorl right," reassuring me, as if I thought it might fly open, suddenly releasing the others. At that moment the yard became flooded with light.

"Moon's up, Charlie," said Baines.

73

"So I see," and there was Joshua stood four square, staring upwards, almost as though the moon's appearance was a transgression.

"You are doing what you want to do, Charlie, I mean you needn't if you don't want to, that is."

My reply was tardy, as I thought to myself, "I suppose I am," feeling suddenly like Baines himself, without will.

How easy it is to be a failure. Baines went on down the yard.

"Here we are," he announced, took a big key from his pocket, and unlocked the door. "There!" and his bulk vanished into the darkness, and I followed. He sounded violent as he searched about for the lamp. It haloed him the moment he lit it.

"Right, Charlie."

"You come out here very often, Mr. Baines?"

"When I can, Charlie. Have to feel like it," and as if I were stone deaf, he shouted, "feel."

I looked about for something to sit on.

"You heard?" he said.

"Heard what, Mr. Baines?"

"'Bout me going out last night, Charlie."

"I could scarcely have *not* heard," I said.

"I did go."

"I gathered that."

"I'd run off now, Charlie, if I could."

"Why don't you? It might change your whole life, Mr. Baines."

"Too late. D'you know 'The Winter Song of the Wind' then?"

"Afraid I don't."

I am not really listening, but staring round and round the Baines den fascinated.

"This is your den?"

"Sright," and he promptly sat himself down, and didn't bother to notice that I must now stand. And I searchlighted the Baines escape hole.

"So this is it," I told myself, "this is how he escapes from Mrs. Baines, from Winifred."

In this common garden shed Baines played the flute, and I hoped that his wish came true, that he played himself right out of the world.

It contained a small wicker table, a strip of carpet, a small bookcase, a hard wooden chair, an empty shelf.

He leaned over me. "My real life, Charlie," he said.

"Your *life?*"

"Sright." He picked up the flute and executed a minor scale.

"Well," I said. "*And* you read, Mr. Baines," and I bent down to examine the contents of the bookcase. He rose, stood behind me.

"Not really," he said, hovering over me with the lamp.

"Good Lord," I exclaimed, and began reading aloud the various titles. "What's this. *The Mastery of the Self. Well!* Interesting, Mr. Baines, very interesting—*I* say, *The Love Poems of Lord Byron*—*his* fiery thoughts—oh, no—no, no, no, Mr. Baines," and I burst out laughing. "No, not——" and I read aloud, " 'How to breed Canaries'—you don't mean, well——" and for some reason I just couldn't stop laughing.

"Don't laugh, Charlie," Baines said.

"Sorry, Mr. Baines."

His whisper was just audible. "I am glad of that, Charlie."

"Fancy! *The History of Hydraulics*, in *four* volumes," and I lowered my voice. "And these catalogues, Mr. Baines, hundreds of them."

"Used to collect them one time, Charlie," he said.

"I see. Well, are you going to play something for me now?"

"All right. Won't stop too long then, s'cold in here."

"It is rather."

He put the lamp on the table, and I stood near to this, considering it offered the only warmth.

"How long do you stay here when you come?" I asked.

"S'long as I feel like it, Charlie, course you have to *feel*."

"I do understand."

"Thanks then, Charlie."

He picked up the flute, and then himself. "You sit, Charlie, I like standing when I play," and I sat down.

Suddenly there was a wild flutter of notes from the flute.

Looking at Baines, I could only think in terms of worlds. *This* one, the one outside, Winifred's, Mrs. Baines's. Baines cleared the flute, and then his throat.

"I don't want to keep you here *too* long, Mr. Baines," I said.

"She'll call, Charlie, always calls when she thinks I've had enough."

"Then play," I said.

And the failure played, out of his big mouth, and out of his wooden head. The shed vanished, the yard, the house. I sat back in the chair, my eyes resting on this man, huge over his delicate instrument, concentrated, and, I hoped, lost. There was something attractive about the faint yellow glow from the lamp, in the very smell of the oil. The shed drowned in music. When I shut my eyes the waves of the sea rose and sank, a valley glittered, and the air tinkled like a bell. Some trees were stiff and bare as winter bone. And in a whole vast sky, a single hovering bird. "The Winter Song" rose up and up, and flooded round and round. When I opened my eyes and looked at Baines, I knew he was saved.

"Beautiful, Mr. Baines, beautiful," I said.

"You really think so, Charlie, then?"

"I do."

Poor Baines, who scarcely knows the moments when they come to him.

"If only you'd play in the house," I said, "it would cheer them up."

His voice was sad. He replied, "Mrs. B. does not like music, Charlie."

"A pity. I suppose it's hard to know what she likes, Mr. Baines."

"She sees her way then, Charlie."

"I'm sure she does."

"Yes."

"I'm sorry for Winifred," I said.

"Are you, Charlie?"

"I'm sorry for you all."

"Why then?"

"It doesn't matter," I said.

"Why then?"

"It's not important. Play again, Mr. Baines. I liked that music."

"What then?"

"The piece you've just played."

"Right then."

I think of the flute as anchor, as rock, as I watch Baines play. And then the voice that shattered the music. I sat up.

"What's that?"

"Only Mrs. B., Charlie, not to worry, she always calls, I told you that."

"Just a moment," I said, and I went to the door of the shed.

It seemed unbelievable, a window had opened in this house, and now I could hear clear upon the night air the heavy voice of Mrs. Baines.

"Mr. Baines. Are *you* there then, Bainesy?"

A window *opened*. In *this* house. I shut the door quickly and returned to my seat.

"It was Mrs. Baines," I said.

The flute was lying on the table, and Baines was standing

there, not looking at anything in particular, and perhaps not thinking anything very important either. "You heard?" he said.

"I did. And it's almost time for you to go in, Mr. Baines."

He came over, put his hands on my shoulder.

"If they'd only love each other, Charlie, I'd be happy," he said.

"Would you, *really*?"

"I would, lad, I would, 'sfact. Often pray for that, 'sno use, nothing comes, saddens me here then, Charlie," and a big finger pressed upon his left breast.

"Do you love Mrs. Baines?" I asked. "Sorry, I shouldn't have said that, please forget it."

He gave a shrug of the shoulders, but made no reply. The fingers of one hand played with the flute.

Suddenly he threw wide his arms, looked helplessly at me, and exclaimed, "You see how it is, Charlie?"

"How what is?"

"Things, Charlie, just things."

"Yes, but what, Mr. Baines?"

"Every day the same," he said.

Everything the same in this house, forever and forever. No change. Day grinding into day, one night wearing out another, and the world shut rudely out. The Baines expression is serious, and his bulk is close again.

"Never get away from what you are, Charlie, 'sfact."

"Don't I know."

"Are you coming then, Mr. B.?"

"There she is again," he said.

"And you are going, Mr. Baines?"

"Sright, Charlie. What's the use of not."

I hadn't a clue myself, and now I conveyed to Baines that it was far too cold to remain any longer.

"Righto then. Glad you came, Charlie," he said.

78

"This then is the *whole* of your life, Mr. Baines. This shed, that flute, that kitchen, your room upstairs, giving her what she likes best, hammering them in at Lawler's."

"Sright, Charlie," he replied, and as though determined that it was, he picked up the lamp and blew it out. We stood together in the darkness.

"Is there no place for *you*, anywhere?"

"Too late, Charlie. Too late."

"My God!"

"What's that?"

"Nothing."

"Half a minute, Charlie," and he put his stout shoulder against the jammed door. "There, we're out."

I wanted to laugh again, say "So we are", but didn't, and followed him into the yard. When I looked up the window was still open.

"Charlie!" he said, and caught my arm.

"Yes?"

"Are *you* never coming then, Bainesy?"

"It doesn't matter, no, it doesn't matter," he said, and walked to the kitchen door. I stood for a moment to look at the moon. Somehow I felt more than glad that it was there. I went in behind Baines.

"Lock up, Mr. B."

"I am locking up," wearily.

"And see to the windows before you come up then."

"I will see to the windows, Mrs. B."

A roar from Mrs. Baines came down like a spear. "You there, Charlie?"

"I'm here."

"Did *he* show you his wounds, Charlie?"

I looked at Baines, he looked at me. He put his hand to his mouth.

"Did he? Was he sorry for himself, did he ask you to stroke

that head of his, did he tell you what a terrible life he has, did he say anything about her in the front room? Well then, Charlie?"

"We talked about nothing. Mr. Baines played his flute, and I listened!"

"I'll put it in his coffin when the time comes, Charlie."

Baines stood motionless. I whispered in his ear.

"I must go up now, Mr. Baines. I must drop a line to my mother."

"You said that last night, Charlie," he whispered back.

"I meant to but didn't manage it."

"Better go up then, Charlie," he said. "Good night, sleep well then."

"I will," I said, and crept to the bottom of the stairs. He followed.

"I suppose she's asleep by now," I said.

"Who then?"

"Winifred."

His concern was great. "Oh God, Charlie, I only hope she is. Sometimes, in the night, she wakes up, bad then, always is. Sometimes she goes searching for something in the Book, don't know what, really, but she does."

"But she doesn't——"

"She did once, Charlie. Come into our room, yes indeed, made Mrs. B. get out of bed, go on her knees, pray for forgiveness."

"And you? What did you do, Mr. Baines?"

"I was between them, what could I do then, Charlie?"

"But this thing can't go on, surely, Mr. Baines, I mean——"

"It will, Charlie, it will," and his words were cold as well as leaden.

"I *must* go up to my room," I thought, "now."

"What are you two talking about down there then?"

"Nothing, Mrs. B. Nothing."

"Are you sure?"

There seemed no answer to that. I made a noisy ascent of the stairs, rattled the door knob, went in, slammed the door after me.

"This is a madhouse," I thought.

"That you, Charlie?"

"It is."

"Had everything you want then?"

"Everything. Thanks. Good night."

"Bainesy'll be up early in the morning, and so will I, Charlie."

Shouting from one room to the other has ceased being odd.

"Satisfied then?"

"*Yes.*"

"No need to shout then."

"Sorry, Mrs. Baines."

"Sorl right then. Where on earth is that *man?*" and the roar renewed. "Mr. B. Are you coming up then, are you?"

"Coming up now, Mrs. B."

"And don't wake the whole *street*, the way you will *clump*, Mr. Baines."

When Baines treads, the house shakes, and now, as he reached the top I could hear the heavy breathings, and after the closed door, a sudden silence. In a moment I had forgotten them. I was thinking of Winifred, seeing her in my mind's eye, clutched and clutching in her polar bed. Does Winifred dream? Does she walk out to Garlan Road, bend to the sleeper, ache for the resurrection, bare her breast, cry against the stone? That front room has now become for me the *depths* of the house. I think of a force there that will not leave her alone. I think of her turning and turning on the wheel of some terrible limitation. The silence is long, unusual. I listen, my head close to the wall. Are they sleeping? Or are they listening? Perhaps Mrs. Baines is as yet uncertain about those doors, that window. Is everything secure, safe.

"Bainesy?"

"Well, Mrs. B.?"

And I knew they were not asleep.

"Did you notice her?"

"Notice who, Mrs. Baines?"

"Who'd you think then. *Her.*"

"Well?"

"Huggin' him with her eyes, Bainesy. You *must* be blind."

4

The creaking door woke me up. "Who's that?"

Not a sound. "I must be dreaming," I thought.

A child-like voice saying, "Charlie."

I sat up, listening. Why rest. Why try to. Why *sleep*?

"Who is that?"

"Me," so softly I had to strain to listen.

And under my breath I exclaimed, "Who?"

"*Me*," a little louder.

"Damn!" and I switched on the light. The doorknob moved, the door.

"Who *is* it?" a fierce whisper.

"Me, Charlie."

I got out of bed, I had to. I went to the door just as Winifred came in.

"You?"

"Me, Charlie."

She was almost lost within the folds of the blanket. I was angry, and I was sick of it.

"Well?"

"Did they——"

I lost control. "*No*. They did *not*."

"You don't know what I was going to say, Charlie."

"I *know*. And I'm *sick* of it. I shall leave here to-morrow."

She cowered against the wall. I sat down on the bed.

"What is it? Why have you come, Winifred? Do you know

83

the time? I've only just got off to sleep myself. They talked their heads off in there. Nobody seems to sleep or even want to. But *I* do. Well now?"

"They told you, didn't they. Told you I was mad. I heard them."

"Nobody said anything," I said.

She began to cry.

"Please," I said. "You'll wake them. Please go back to bed, Winifred."

"D'you think I'm mad, Charlie?"

"No, I don't. Is that all right? Will that *do*?"

I went to her, took her by the arm, gently led her towards the door.

"Please. Do go back to bed. It's very late."

"Hear everything that goes on in this house, Charlie, they were talking to you."

"Not about you. Will you please *go*."

She trembled under my hand. I opened the door. "Come along now."

"Charlie!"

"Well?"

"You don't really, do you?"

"For God's *sake*," I said.

"She——"

"Get *out*."

I hated this house, I hated her, I hated myself.

"Are you *going*?"

And then I was sorry. I took her arm, led her to the bed, and she sat down. "There! Just be quiet. Say nothing. Just sit there," and I sat beside her.

"That *bitch*," she cried, and covered her face with her hands. She sobbed bitterly.

"Listen," I said. "Listen to me."

"*Do* you think I am, Charlie, they're always talking about

me, they only want to get me out of the house, that's it, Charlie, it *is*."

"You *are* mad. Will that do? Now get *out*," and I pulled her clear of the bed, pushed her towards the door. "Go back to your room."

And I shut her out. "Poor Winifred," I thought, and got back to bed.

It was only when I switched out the light that I realized she was still outside the door. I got up again, silently opened it. And there she was, a crumpled heap on the top stair. Winifred crouched to Winifred.

"My God! I shouldn't have said that, I shouldn't."

She drew herself up, went slowly down the stairs.

"I'll go down to her," I told myself. "There's nothing else to do."

I heard her door close. I heard the Baines snores. I heard the clock strike. I went in and dressed. I crept slowly down, and went into the cold hall. I stood outside her door.

"Winifred!"

I waited. Can she hear? Can't she? I fumbled with the knob, the door opened, and there she was. "Winifred," I said.

She sat motionless on the bed, clutching the blanket tightly about her. "Winifred. I'm sorry."

She did not hear, or did not want to. There was no light, save that thrown from a nearby lamp's reflection. The silence itself seemed black.

"I'm sorry. Can I come in?"

"What for?"

"Can I come *in*?"

We are both strangers.

"Go away."

"I only want to explain," I said.

"I know now."

"You *don't* know," I said.

"Go away. I'll *scream*."

"Please."

"I don't want to see you any *more*."

When she rose I drew back. "Please, Winifred," I said.

The door slammed in my face. But I stood there, waiting. After a minute or two I knocked.

"Winifred."

No answer.

"*Winifred*."

Not a sound. Again I opened the door, looked in. There she was. What is she waiting for? The end of the world? A beginning? Or just for Tom? Perhaps he will walk down the street, peer through the window. "I *am* sorry."

"There's something I want to say to you, Winifred. Can I come in?"

At last she spoke. "If I'm mad, Charlie, what shall I do?"

"Come out with me," I said.

"Where then?"

"Out. Just out," and I entered the room. "I'm sorry, Winifred, forgive me, but you did wake me up, so suddenly, at first I thought I'd been dreaming. Really. Can I sit down?"

"Do what you want to do," she said, and turned towards the window.

"I want to talk to you," I said. "I want you to come out with me. *Now*. This very minute. Will you? For a walk. *Out*side. We can't talk here, nobody can. Will you come?"

She stares in, stares out. Has she heard? Does she want to? Can she feel my breath down the back of her neck? Are her thoughts knotted, strangling her.

"*Winifred*."

86

And at last she turned and looked at me.

"Come for a walk now, Winifred."

"What for?"

"I want to. Will you come?"

When she stood up, I said quite casually, "I'll wait in the hall. Get dressed."

"I am dressed."

She flung off the blanket, and there she was, dressed. Does she ever *un*dress?

Does *she* sleep in her clothes, sit in that window night *and* day?

"They'll hear."

"They *won't*."

Money will save Mrs. Baines, and "The Winter Song" will often be about Joshua's shoulders. But Winifred?

"Come *now*."

"Where, Charlie, *where*?" low in her throat, desperate, always desperate.

"*Out!* Into the world, Winifred. I'll wait for you. Have you a key?"

"Only Mr. B. has the key."

"Then the back way. I'll wait for you by the wall. Hurry."

The cold green hall is colder, and the draughts lift up the linoleum. The Baines snores beat through the bedroom door, float down the stairs, fill the hall. Winifred came out.

I whispered in her ear. "This way."

"Where?" Unready, confused.

For a single moment the sudden dread that the *parrot* might hear, wake powerfully, screech the Baineses out of their deep sea.

"Through here, Winifred."

"Yes, Charlie," and suddenly, her hand in mine.

"Ssh!"

"Hush," she said.

In the kitchen I paused, and there was a single glow from the dark mass of the everlasting fire, like an eye watching.

"Ssh!"

Across a yard, past *his* hole, under the moon that is as bright as ever.

"Where are we going then?"

"Into the world."

"Ssh!"

And there we were, intent in a flash, so *ready*, and I fumbling with bolt and catch.

"There's an entry here," I said.

"All jowlers round here."

"Jowlers?"

"Sright, Charlie, jowlers," and then the door opened. I held my breath, expecting the squeak, but none came; the door moved backwards on oiled wheels.

"There, Winifred," I said, gripping her hand, "we're out."

"Christ! Where am I?"

"Out. Safe. This way."

The world is vast. Where shall I lead Winifred?

"Where am I going, Charlie?"

She stopped dead, stiffened, in the long entry, leaned to the wall. Under a moon it seemed mountains high.

"Anywhere," I said, "anywhere that is away from the *house*," and I felt as if I had driven teeth into the word. The words came tumbling down at me. Prison, bedlam, sad, lost, laughable, hopeless. We walked away, one behind the other, for Winifred's "jowler" is long and narrow.

"Oh Christ, Charlie," and she stopped again, flung herself against the wall. I put my arms round her, gently pulled.

"Nothing is strange, Winifred. We've just come out into the world, that's all. It's fast asleep. There's nothing to be afraid of."

The heap at the wall is inert, the hands raised, the fingers spread, clutching. Looking at her I could only think of feet in the silence, a stranger suddenly *headlong* in our direction, a rude halt, and a ruder ultimatum.

"Who are *you*? Why are you *here*?"

I stared at Winifred. Such fear, such wounds, such dimensions. And I, too, leaned with her, pressed against this high, and seemingly endless, wall, wishing the moon dead. Damn Baines. Damn Mrs. Baines. What shall I do with Winifred? Take her forcibly by the arm, dragging her after me, out, far out to Garlan Road. Shall I? And put the question? The last one. To him.

Leave her alone. Leave her *alone*.

"Winifred!"

I hardly realized I had spoken, and the clutched form moved.

"What, Charlie, what?"

Under this high wall, under this curious patch of light and shadow, the child crowned Winifred. An ocean of trust. I can take Winifred to hell, poor, simple, tormented Winifred.

"This way," and I waited.

"Come now," I said, my hand on her arm, pulling again. "Come *on*."

I had to pull hard. "This way."

"What for?"

"Just let's get out of this entry," I said.

Farther away from the house, farther and farther.

"One day, Winifred, or perhaps one night, Mr. Baines *will* go, and then there will only be Mrs. Baines left."

Winifred came away from the wall, and she has never been closer.

"And Mrs. Baines. She'll die."

"Will she?"

"I'm sure she will."

"Charlie!"

I put my fingers on her mouth, I whispered into her ear.

"We're all of us a little mad, Winifred, didn't you know that?"

And then we were clear of that entry, the towering wall. It *had* ended. Our footsteps rang out sharp and clear on the night air.

"Look at the world," I said, and she looked at the world.

"When were you last out?"

"Last Sunday."

"You were out this morning, too. Don't you remember?"

"Sorry, Charlie, I forgot," she said.

"Of *course*."

We walked on and on, up and up.

"Where are you taking me, Charlie?"

"Out of the town. Up *there*."

She hung on my arm, as weight, as curious loss. At the top of the street, we stopped. I turned Winifred round.

"There it is," I said, "all of it. Fast asleep. We're going on."

"Where then?"

"Up *there*!"

How strange to look down on the dead town, listen to the silence. Doors are closed, buildings huddle, and Joshua's "many feet" are far away.

"It's all right. Come on."

Yet I didn't move, but found myself staring into Winifred's eyes. And I thought of the tiny part of us that drives, that hates us. Nearer and nearer to the old quarry. Scrambling over the loose stones.

"I've forgotten my watch, Winifred."

"What then?"

"Nothing," I said, "keep walking."

"Where then, Charlie?"

"Away from the house," I said.

The broken ground about us seems to suck in the light. She stopped again.

"Come on, Winifred. This way now," I said.

I felt my arm gripped. "When Tom was——" and I wanted to shout out, "*Kill* him. *Again*."

"Talk, Winifred."

Has she heard me?

"Talk *now*," I said.

"Charlie!"

"*Talk*."

"What shall I say then?"

"Anything. What you can't say in the house."

A cloud struck the moon, darkened us.

"What's that?"

"Your *life*."

"He——"

"*Your* life, Winifred, *yours*. Tell me about it. Nobody will hear, only me. The house is down *there*, lost with the others. Why did you come to my room?"

"They were talking about me, I knew they were."

"They were *not*. I listened, too. I heard. They were talking about themselves, Winifred. They love themselves too much to talk about anyone else. Didn't you know that?"

"No then, I didn't."

"*Forget* them, for once, *now*."

"They talk about you, Charlie."

"I didn't hear them."

"They do."

She began to shiver. "Here, take my coat. There. We'll go this way."

"Which way then?"

"*Right* through the town."

"I want to go back," she said.

"We are going back," I said.

"Proving room at Lawler's used to say there was no bed big enough for her."

"For *who*?"

"Mrs. B., of course."

She stopped again, jerked herself free.

"It's all *right*. It's only a clock striking," I said. "Come along now. We are going back. To your room. You love your room, don't you? You won't be happy until you're behind that door. Mr. Baines is just the same. I had to drag him out this morning, just for a short stroll, and he was on edge the whole time, and was soon on the way home again. I've never met people that loved a house so much. The house seems to own you."

"He always brought me flowers, Saturdays, Charlie," she said.

"I've been meaning to write a letter to my mother ever since I arrived, and I'm still writing it," I said.

"When Tom came to us *her* eyes were daggers any time."

"She'll be getting worried if I don't write soon. My mother *hates* North, Winifred. Thinks it a very odd place indeed. Do you think it's strange, Garlston, for instance. Well, take your house, take Baptist Street. When I go up or down I always watch the curtains. Now I know there's nothing behind them except mice."

"Even Bainesy said to me, 'Watch her then, you know what she is.' I used to like her once, my *sister*, Charlie."

A street is hilly, the descent rapid, heavy feet in the distance strike sparks from cobbles. A policeman.

"I stuck a pen in a solicitor's directory, Winifred, just for the fun of it, and here I am. Just imagine it. Walking with you through Garlston at one o'clock in the morning."

"I've lived in my head ever since, Charlie. He lives there too, *really*."

"And when I got here I just couldn't find a room anywhere. A pure accident that I found your sister's advert in the *Church Gazette*. I was in the Public Library. If you'd seen me, Winifred, poring over those newspapers with the rest of them. I was lucky to find your place. Mrs. Baines said space is more valuable than gold up here, and I agree."

"I told her then, Charlie, 'I'll *never* forgive you, *never*.' Nor I won't. I loved Tom. *Loved* him."

Twice she disdained my arm, and once suddenly ran off, and I had to run after her. Now I took it again, and I could feel her trembling violently.

"It's all right. We're going back to the house," I said.

"There was a man beside me, Winifred, in that Library, he was reading *The Times*. You should have seen his *eyes*. I had an idea he might have been standing there for two or three days, perhaps even *dead*, so erect, so *still*. And just staring, and finger-tips like drawing-pins, *right* through the paper——"

"Even after the bitch did what she did that night, having him on her bed no less, bold as brass, even then that big slob said to me, he said, 'Try to forgive her, Winifred, try, because if you *don't*, you can't *live*. World's no use to you.' That's what the silly man said, Charlie——"

"That whole reading room was the strangest country, Winifred. The silence was suspended in the air like the very sword of Damocles. A country of snufflings and sneezings, and overcoats, and bent heads, and exhausted watery eyes behind bits of glass, and then, suddenly in the midst of all that, the most *shattering* interruption from a man in the far corner by the door. 'In the name of Christ,' he shouted, 'and what are things coming to.' You should have seen the faces *then*, and that rush for the door."

"Charlie!"

I'm not really listening, not wanting to, the whole thing's too odd, lurching down hilly streets, this turning of corners, this sudden halting, this going on, and Tom between us, inside her skull, locked in her belly, pressed to her heart, the unforgettable, undying Tom, who spread himself out in Baptist Street, in all his weakness, in a surge of Northern passion.

"*This* way," I said, "not that, *and* you've told me nothing, *nothing*."

"Charlie!" so quietly, so casually, where on earth *is* she?

"*Winifred*."

Somewhere a chain was pulled, and a dog barked, and then we stopped *again*, another corner.

"Charlie!"

"What? *Well?* What now?"

I cannot hide a growing irritation.

" 'Yes,' he said to me, afternoon after we saw Mr. Belpin about tying us up, 'yes, Winifred, dear, you'll have what you want, don't worry. We'll wed at Whit.' "

"What the *hell* are you talking about, Winifred?"

She exploded. "About *him*."

"What about him?"

"You don't understand, Charlie."

"I don't."

"I wish I was dead."

"Don't *shout*."

"I'm not shouting," she said, and shouted.

"You *are*. You'll wake the whole *town*."

I clapped my hand over her mouth. She has the feel of an engine, vibrating under my arm.

"There! Take it *easy*, control yourself. Don't worry. And if you mention *him* again, I'll think you *are* mad."

"Sorry, Charlie. I am, really. I can't help it."

"*Try*. You *can*."

"Wish he'd taken me away *then*," she said.

I halted, clapped my hand over her mouth again. "Ah—ah——"

94

And then we walked on. "Would've——"

"No. *No.*"

"Come on. Let's go down this street, I'll show you the office where I have to start work to-morrow. There's a Mr. Greele there, Winifred, and I had to interview him as soon as I arrived. I thought it was a pub, glazed brick, that sort of thing. Anyhow, I found my way into the enquiry office, and sat there waiting for him. It was funny, I must tell you about it. I wasn't thinking about anything in particular when suddenly the door burst open, and there was a tall, thin, grey-looking gent, with a shiny bald head. He stared at me, and said, 'Well?'

" 'Good morning, sir,' I said. 'I'm Mr. Elston. Charles Elston.'

"Somebody came down the corridor, and the moment he passed Mr. Greele, Greele shouted after him, 'And tinge it with terror, Mr. Henge.' They were the very first words I heard in that office. Mr. Greele came in, and closed the door. He stood over me. He then pointed violently towards the door, and exclaimed, 'What did you think of that, Mr.—er—er— I've forgotten the name. Now there's a woman been written to seven times, *seven*, and doesn't seem to know even *now* whether she is or is not married. Think of that, Mr.—er——'

" 'Elston, sir.'

" 'Some people don't seem to grow up, Elston, you *are* Elston, until you've got them on their knees.' He then sat down beside me.

" 'Elston, Charles Elston,' he said. 'Why of course. I remember now. Incidentally your mother wrote to me about you. She asks me to look after you, Mr.—er—it *is* Elston. H'm! I'm afraid the North is not a blanket, Mr.—er——'

" 'Elston, sir. E. l. s. t. o. n.' I had to say it five times, Winifred, before it sank in."

I turned and looked at Winifred.

"You weren't even listening," I said.

"Did you say something then, Charlie?"

"*Not* a word. Not a single word. Round this corner. There it is. At last."

"What, Charlie?"

"The entry. The en—*try*," right into her ear.

And I pushed her into the long, narrow cavern.

"Now you're safe."

"You think we're odd, don't you then, Charlie?"

"Why should I? Why *shouldn't* you sit in the parlour window for the rest of your life? Why *shouldn't* your sister save and save? Why shouldn't Mr. Baines run away if he wants to? What's odd about it, well, what is *odd*?"

"Oh!" and she stared at me, open-mouthed. "Oh!"

"We'd better get along," I said. "I know you're only too anxious to get back to the rack. You love the rack, don't you, Winifred? Love lying on it."

"We're nearly home, Charlie."

"I noticed that."

"Me and him used to——"

"And a precious view *you've* had of the world. What did you see? Tell me, Winifred?"

"He couldn't look at me after it happened, Charlie, s'truth, so ashamed he was. Was all I had, really."

Tom clung and clung and I said nothing. We reached the back door. She turned again, looked me full in the face, her own now beautifully clear as the cloud passed. "D'you think they're asleep?"

"How do I know *that*?"

I lifted the latch, pushed in the door, and always Winifred is close.

"There! Ssh!" We moved quietly across the yard, and our shadows were ten feet long. Suddenly I put my mouth against her ear.

"If Mrs. Baines died to-morrow, Winifred, you'd be glad, wouldn't you?"

But one question is only followed by another one. There are no answers.

"D'you think we're all wrong then, Charlie?"

Her hands rest on my arms, she looks up again, waiting.

"I said you'd have nothing to hate, if your sister died to-morrow."

We stand by Joshua's haven, the dark shed, Baines's secretless secret, and I thought of a striving for calm, the fugitive content.

"Much that we do's wrong, Winifred, but there's always someone around to tell us we're right, and we're all weak——"

"Charlie?"

"What?"

And then the low explosion, the engine throbbing again, something leaping in her arm as she caught my own.

"Let me get in, let me get in, *now*."

"You'd have *nothing* to hate, I *said* it, and you haven't even the answer. Have you?"

"Bainesy wouldn't mind. He never minds anything, Charlie."

"I'm talking to *you*."

"Are you then?"

I said nothing, there seemed nothing I could say, and I pushed at the kitchen door. And fiercely under my breath, feeling like Winifred, wanting to be in, quickly, up in my room, the door fast, *alone*.

"All *right*. The front room's still there, waiting for you, like a friend. The bed's waiting, you can lie on it forever."

For a moment she hesitated, and I pushed again, harder this time.

"Go *on*. You wanted to get back, you're *back*."

"Isn't the fire just lovely, Charlie, then?"

"Isn't it."

"He used to sit in that chair, Charlie, see him now, *so* comfortable. Oh, God! I wish he'd taken me away *then*."

And through my teeth: "And *why* didn't he? To the other end of the world."

"You don't understand nothing, Charlie."

"I *know*. I'm *glad*. And I'm leaving here first thing in the morning."

She gripped the fireguard, stared into the smouldering mass.

"If only he had," she said, her voice low, suddenly calm, and I knew she was off on another journey. "I *wish* he had."

"So do I."

"Do you then?"

"*Yes*."

I, too, leaned on the fireguard, stared into the fire. It made me think of volcanoes. Instinctively I found myself listening for the Baines snores. They were doing their duty. We spoke in whispers.

"Aren't you going to your room?" I asked.

She had seated herself in the big armchair, her head a little forward, her restless fingers turning and twisting at the cloth of her very plain skirt.

"I wish I was dead," she said.

"You could have forgiven her," I said.

The shout was quite unexpected. "*Who?*"

"You'll wake the house. Ssh! Couldn't you have forgiven her?"

"I couldn't," and the voice seemed to come as from some great distance.

"All right, you couldn't, and I don't want to hear one more word about Tom. Understand? Do you *understand?*"

She refuses to answer, refuses to look. I listen again, for

movements upstairs. Did they hear that sudden frantic shout?
Or have they heard it so often that it no longer matters?

"Winifred, one day you'll be alone, you *will*."

"I can always go and talk to him, Charlie."

"He's *dead*."

"Not really, Charlie, he talks to me Sundays."

"Is *that* why you drag them out there every week?"

"Mind out of my *way*," she said.

She walked out of the kitchen, and this time left the
door wide open. When the call came, I stiffened. It was
Baines.

"Winifred!"

"Good God! They have heard," I thought, and immediately
made for the stairs. I removed my shoes, and went quietly
up.

"Wini—*fred*!"

I managed to open my door without a sound, and for some
reason found myself holding on to the doorknob waiting.

"*Wini*fred!"

And then I went in, but did not fully close the door. The
slightest sound now . . .

"Our *Winifred*!"

"What the hell am I doing here? In this house? Standing
in the darkness, afraid to move, one way or the other. And
listening, always listening. Oh, *God*! I wish I could *laugh*."

I pulled back the bedclothes, removed coat and hat, lay
quietly down. And the bed did not creak.

"She *is* mad. They're all of them mad. I might just as well
have stayed in, got that letter off to mother. I simply *must*
get it off to-morrow."

In the next room the bed suddenly groaned.

"To-morrow. Good heavens! I haven't given it a thought.
I *must* see if Greele and Grimes can help."

"Are you sitting up then, Mrs. Baines?"

"Of course I'm sitting up, Bainesy. *You* heard."

"It's two o'clock, Mrs. B."

"I know it is. And why should you lie down then if I can't."

"You *can't*?"

"Didn't you hear then, Mr. B. Didn't you? *I* did."

When the bed groaned again I knew that Baines, too, was sitting up.

"Heard what then?"

"Them."

"*Who?*"

"Who'd you suppose, Mr. B.? Her and Charlie."

"What about her then?"

"She's been out, Mr. Baines. Think of *that*. Her that hates going out any time 'cept Sundays when she drags us after her, the bitch, and one of these days, Bainesy, she'll get such a surprise, such a surprise."

"Well then?"

"She'll find Lazarus had a brother after *all*, Bainesy, shake her that will, if she could *only* get under the bloody flowers Sundays she'd get, aye, and wouldn't mind if he dragged her in neither. Are *you* listening?"

"Mrs. B. For the love of Christ! Sometimes your tongue drives me to the unforbiddable sources, it does, Mrs. B., *and* I'm telling you——"

The roar that followed shook the house.

"And I'm telling you he's been out. So's she. At this time of the night. He's *had* her, that's what."

"Had her?"

"Course he has, what d'you think, well then, shake your head, Mr. B., for God's sake, shake it, find out where you *are*, here, by *me*, what's telling you something happened, seems to me that Charlie's took her off somewhere this night and maybe blew out the light in her head, s'fact, Bainesy, s'fact. Heard them talking down there just now, while you were snoring your head off, and dreaming, I suppose, *and* the usual one, getting away from here, that's it, then isn't it? Well, the world's not a big Christmas card, Bainesy, and don't you ever go thinking it is. Never was. Learn *that*. Sides, what'd you expect from anyone's come from where he has, and d'you notice anything *ever* in your lifetime, Mr. B., tell me *that* then, knew soon's I saw him, and all that bloody nonsense about us down here leaning on everything, 'n the way he looks at you sometimes, bet you didn't notice then, did you, well *did* you. *I* don't mind who has her, really, but *he* has, this very night, certain of it, Mr. B., and it's up to you *now* to go in and ask him all about that. Hear me then? Light in her head she is, and always was, but Charlie's put a fine little seed into her, I'm sure of that, won't do her any harm, of *course*, what harm would it do any woman anyhow since they's always feeling the lack, and that's why I'm so very fond of you, Bainesy, *very* fond of you, you know where to bestow peace any time."

"Mrs. B."

"Well?"

"What could I say to him then, and who can be sure, Mrs. Baines?"

"*If* you said something very natural to Charlie, it'd shake him. *You* ask him straight out *now*, Bainesy. 'Have you had our Winifred on her back?' What's the use of struggling to find out anything in this world, except directly."

A silence, and then a long, low sigh from Baines.

"Are you listening to me, Mr. B.?"

"Aren't I always listening to you, Mrs. Baines? Well, aren't I? Aren't I always doing what you ask, and often for the love of Christ, the sake of peace. *Aren't* I always giving?"

"See him now. That's what. And there is the money side, you *know* that. You're so very fond of saving people, Bainesy, well then? Her being half mad as she is our Winifred mightn't even notice she was being saved, but you have your duty, you have."

"Mrs. B., I have told you once, and I will tell you again. We are *all* damned. *Damned.* In this house. I couldn't save Winifred from anything, so leave her be then, leave her be, s'happy in her window, 'n' the empty house isn't the only thing she sees out there neither. She has her little view of glory, Mrs. B. Let her sail her sea, and if she's joined by another, a little one, let her embrace what'll come to her. Even the damned may pull on a little happiness, Mrs. Baines. *You* know that."

"But he won't stay now, you know it, threw me a hint this morning. You know he thinks we're queer——"

"Queer?"

"Queer, Mr. B. *Queer.*"

"I won't be rushed, Mrs. B."

"S'pity that, 'n it's made me think sudden about your lot— I mean your parents, Bainesy. Seems like they didn't want to be too rushed neither, and look at the result, I could light the fire for a year just from the wood in your head. Are you going in to him or aren't you?"

"Let me think, Mrs. B. Easy now. Suppose you're wrong then?"

"I am not wrong, Mr. B. Come on then, do something about her. Go and talk to him, who ever heard of a mad creature being took out into a night town like that, 'n' so secret too, I tell you it's done. D'you hear what I'm saying, Mr. Baines?"

Baines yawned. "I have to get up early in the morning, you know that. And it's getting on three o'clock, did you know *that*?"

"Sright, I did notice."

"I'll talk to him in the morning."

"Now, Mr. B. *Now.* You'll get nowt off him if he cools, nothing. Probably still panting, Bainesy, that's the time to go in. Are you going *in* then?"

"I'm not, Mrs. B. And that will surprise you."

"*I* never allowed anything to surprise me, Bainesy, never. Why, mother'd turn in her grave if she thought I had."

The sudden thud made me jump.

"Heavens," I thought, "she's pushed him out of bed."

And now I could hear his clumsy, heavy movements about the room.

"Are *you* moving then?"

"Oh, all right, *all* right."

"The noise you can make, Bainesy, just going from here to there, the *noise.* Wouldn't be surprised if Charlie wasn't listening to us, s'not the first time neither, I expect, and if you went down to *her* very suddenly you'd find her curled up like a squirrel, and very happy, I'm sure, very happy."

"I'm going—*now.*"

I heard the door open, and Baines come out. And after that, the shout.

"And everything's to be paid for, Bainesy, everything in this world. Tell him that."

"I will, Mrs. B."

"Then hurry up then."

"I am."

I heard the feet outside my door, and then the gentle tapping. "Are you awake there, Charlie?"

So low in his throat, so softly, it was difficult to credit Baines with such a beautiful pianissimo. I did not answer. I felt sorry for the will-less man, and now his heavy, tortured breathings gave me an uncomfortable feeling. What should I say?

"Charlie!"

"Are *you* gone in to him, then, Mr. B.?"

I heard Baines creep back to his own door, open it. "Asleep, Mrs. Baines. Fast, I think. Not a sound. Perhaps it'd be better if I spoke to him in the morning then——"

"Must I go in then, do what you can't, you're so soft, Bainesy. *Wake* him."

"Very well," he said, and the feet pattered back again.

"Charlie! Charlie! Are you asleep then?"

"Why should I be asleep, Mr. Baines? Why should *anybody* be asleep in this house?"

"Awake then, Charlie."

"Well?"

"S'about our Winifred?"

"*What* about *your* Winifred?"

"Mrs. B. heard you go out with her, Charlie, she thinks you had her, did you have her then?"

"*Have* her?"

"Sright."

"We went for a walk, Mr. Baines."

"Where then?"

"Into the world."

"The world, Charlie?"

"That's right."

"What happened *then*?"

"*Nothing*. We just went for a walk round the town, and came home again. The dream palaces were closed, Mr. Baines, and the dances, dogs, and devils were fast asleep. Once, I wished you were with us."

"Mrs. B. says you think we're queer, Charlie. Is that right?"

"Not at all. Why should I think you're queer, Mr. Baines. Any of you?"

There was a roar from the next room. "Are *you* gone in then, Bainesy?"

"No, I haven't. Just talking to him, Mrs. B. Outside his door."

"And now, Mr. Baines," I called softly, "now, if you'll excuse me, I simply must write a letter to my mother——"

"*Now*, Charlie? D'you know what time it is, nearly half-past two in the morning."

"*Now*, Mr. Baines."

"Can I come in then?"

"No. You *cannot* come in, Mr. Baines."

"Were you asleep then, Charlie? Sorry I woke you then."

"*Asleep?*"

"You went out the back way, she heard you, Charlie."

"That's right. We went down something called a jowler, Mr. Baines. And a very long, dark one it was."

"Had her in the entry then?"

I turned over, face to the wall, and I did not answer.

"Charlie?"

"I'll see Charlie in the morning, Bainesy. You come back to bed then."

I heard him moving away from the door, and his own shut behind him.

"I shouldn't worry about him having her out like that, Mr. B., 'cept there is the money side to it. Is to everything, I wonder if he'd take her away with him, Bainesy?"

"Move up."

"D'you think he would then?"

"Charlie's actually writing a letter to his mother, Mrs. B., at this time of the morning. Says they were in the entry together, went for a walk round the town then come home again. That's all."

"And if she *did* go, Bainesy, and took her madness with her, then we'd be together at last, just us two, alone, think of that. And think of all the house, Mr. B., all the rooms in it ours, and the kitchen, and sitting by it in the evening, and not having to go upstairs out of her sight to let her have what she wants when she wants it. I used to think it a bit odd us having to leave the kitchen while she ate, Bainesy, but she would have her way. You know that."

"You had your way, Mrs. B."

"My way's best, Bainesy. Keep the roof over your head, and keep close together forever, and save the money against what comes, Mr. Baines. Sometimes I think I hear the footsteps coming after you, and terrible steps they are, terrible, and God knows whose hand on your shoulder telling you it's the last day for you there."

"Where?" and it was a real, anguished shout from Baines.

"Lawlers. Where else d'you think? Things come, Bainesy, they *do* come, and you'll be glad I'm at the back of you, and you'll never starve. And think of being able to use the front room, at last. You could even shift your things in from out there."

There was the sound of snoring, but not for long.

"Are you listening to me, Bainesy, wake up then and listen. S'me as has the sense in this house, always was, she wouldn't care if we both died to-morrow. You *know* that."

Will they ever lie down? Sleep? Shall *I*? Or must I get on with my letter?

"I've a good mind to go in and see Charlie now."

"Now, Mrs. B.? Now?"

"And why should guilt sleep comfortable, Mr. B.? Well?"

"We don't know what happened."

"Where are you going?"

"I am going down for the Book, Mrs. B."

"Don't go near that one."

"I shall leave her alone."

And Baines got up, and went down for the Book. Will they *never* rest?

"Are you awake in there, Charlie?" Mrs. Baines called.

And I longed, and longed for the morning.

"Did our Winifred let you then, Charlie?"

It was a relief to hear Baines on the stairs, and later to hear the words that were final.

"Charlie's fast asleep, Mr. Baines."

"Dropped off then, Mrs. B. He'll *never* get that letter to his mother finished. And now, Mrs. Baines, *please*, let this day end."

A momentary silence, and then the Book that lived.

"Many there be, which say of my soul, there is no help for him in God, Selah. But thou, O Lord, art a shield for me, my glory, and the lifter up of my head. I cried with my voice, and he heard me out of the holy hill, Selah. I laid me down to sleep, I slept. I awakened, for He sustained me. I will not be afraid."

"Amen," Mrs. Baines said.

"Amen," I said to myself, and was glad to.

"I will talk to him proper to-morrow, Mr. B.," Mrs. Baines said, and Baines said nothing.

"And think of it, Bainesy, if she *went*, there'd just be *us*, alone, together, forever and forever, as the Book say."

And Baines said nothing.

"And wherever the room be, Mr. B., whatever the time, day or night, I'd know you were in it, and safe, for me, just me, Bainesy. I like you around *all* the time, all the time, like the Book says, Mr. B., skin to skin—and I——"

And Baines said nothing.

"Sometimes, Bainesy, and I never said this to you before, sometimes I have a dread of the words that will come out of one's mouth, you never know where their journey ends, like waves in the sea, Bainesy, waves in the sea. There was an angel, can't rightly remember his name, as said that sleep was a peace, ah, I often wonder what you are thinking when you're asleep, and ever since you had that dream of going——"

And Baines snored.

The house was suddenly, wonderfully silent. But not for long. The sound from the kitchen came up clearly, distinctly, and it came from the parrot. Even the parrot dreamed. It was almost refreshing.

5

Evening of the shouts.

"Who's that?"

"Me."

"That Charlie then?"

"It is."

"Sure?"

"Sure. Where are you, Winifred?"

"In here."

"They back yet?"

"Not yet."

"They're late."

"She went out snuffling this morning. Catches cold easily."

"I said they're *late*," my voice rising.

" 'S'overtime I expect, Charlie. Trust her to give Mr. B. a push if there's a few extra pennies to be had, you know that, *don't* you?"

I have a vision of Baines hammering in the last nail, of Mrs. Baines giving a final rinse to Mr. Crawley's cup. My corner is dark, and so, I am sure, is Winifred's.

"Did you have a good night, Charlie?"

"Fairly good," I said, "fairly *good*," and louder now.

"They often talk in the night, Charlie."

"I gathered that—I said I gathered *that*."

"Won't be long now, Charlie, s'pect."

"*Thanks.*"

"It must be—— *Char*lie?"

"*Yes?*"

"Wonder what you'd see out of this window if you lived in the parlour."

"I wonder."

"Bill Foulkes just gone past now, Charlie."

"Aren't you cold in there?"

"Never cold."

Supper is on the hob, the table laid, the Book handy. All one waits for is the death of the Lawler day.

"How odd," I thought to myself. "I've hurried back to this house as Baines would hurry back, as though it were merciful, that I was glad to be in. Yet the vividness of the morning is still remembered. Being wakened by Winifred, being called down, being attended to. Being kind to the parrot, eating my breakfast, not looking at Winifred, not wanting to, feeling always the presence, the pressure of this strange woman. And now I sit hugging the warmth of the kitchen. As Joshua says, it holds the heat of hell, but the hall is always cold. I had knocked. Twice. Three times. But the front door had refused to budge. I entered by the rear, climbing the wall, since the back door itself was locked. And not a sound about as I came into the kitchen. But after long minutes, the sudden shout.

"That you, Charlie," and it was.

The night pushes in.

"Busy day then?"

"Busy enough," I said, "busy *enough.*"

"Oh!"

And she is still in one room, and I am in another.

"I simply *must* get that letter off to-day," I told myself. "*Must.*"

The silence arched again. I can hear my own breathing, the

tick of the clock. I turned round involuntarily, and there was the parrot watching me.

"Lawlers are hammering in a hell of a lot of nails to-day," I thought, and every second I expected to hear the well-known thuds, the key in the lock. The warmth of the fire reached out like arms.

"Charlie."

"*Yes?*"

And in spite of everything I forced myself away from the sucking warmth, and stepped into the hall.

"*Yes?*"

"Oh, nothing, really. Just thinking," Winifred said, and I went back to the fire.

"I knocked at the front door three times, Winifred. I said I knocked three *times, and* the back door was locked, too. Had to climb over the wall in the end."

"Did you then?"

"Yes, yes, yes, I *said* it. Three *times.*"

"It's them being late, Charlie, but that's what it is, *really*, bit of overtime, and how she *loves* it. Don't tell them you came over the wall, Charlie, give them both horrible ideas, 's'fact."

"Of *course* not. Aren't you coming into the kitchen, Winifred?"

"No." It seemed definite enough.

The Lawlers day drags to its end, and we are still waiting.

"Know what she's thinking, Charlie, don't you then?"

The thin, thread-like voice sharpens with each utterance.

"No. I don't."

"Well she is then, *hard.*"

"What about—I said what *about?*"

"Us," screeched.

"*Us?*"

"Sright. Heard her talking to him last night, Charlie."

"You heard her? *When?*"

"After you were gone up and I was in here."

"God *Almighty*."

"What's that then?"

"Nothing. Nothing. *Nothing*."

"Oh! Thought you were saying something. Sorry, Charlie."

I flung it out. "So am I," I said, "so am *I*."

"Hide nothing from her, never will."

"Hide nothing from anybody, even the mice in the house, the *mice*."

And I sat on, anxious to hear the sound of those feet, and that voice out of Egypt, or even out of Byzantium. Suddenly the complete absurdity of an evening situation made me rush to the door and call out, "Why waste the *fire*, Winifred, why waste it?"

"Thought I heard them coming, Charlie. Did you hear anything?"

I roared, had to, felt like it. "Heard *nothing*."

"They won't be long, I'm sure."

"I know."

"Charlie?"

"*Well?*"

"D'you think sometimes that life isn't the right thing then?"

"Sometimes it's just a fake, Winifred," and then I laughed.

"Yes," she replied, pausing, groping, perhaps concentrating, "I suppose it is sometimes, Charlie."

"It's half-past six *now*," I said.

"Any second, I'm sure," she replied.

There was a dull roar past the window, as of rushing waters, and then many feet in the street.

"World's coming home again, Charlie."

"I can hear it, *hear* it."

"Like a nice cup of tea then?"

"*No*."

"All right then. S'her fault, really, told you, she pushes hard when the coin's about, can't help it, always his overtime, her money."

"I'm going out shortly—short-*ly*."

"What's that?"

"I didn't say anything, really I didn't."

"Oh!"

"I'm leaving to-morrow, Winifred," I said, "I'm leaving, going *away*."

"Tell her then."

"I *will*."

"Sright."

"Yesterday, Winifred, I said *yesterday*. Mr. Baines told me what he was."

"What is he?"

"A failure—a *fail*-ure."

"Told *you*. Mr. B. never talks to nobody much, Charlie, *no*body."

"All the same he told me," I shouted.

"What's that?"

"Noth*ing*," and *I* screeched too.

"Starving, Charlie, s'pect, she won't be long now, I'm sure."

"I'm going out for my supper."

Silence.

"*Out*."

Silence.

"Did *you* go out to-day?"

"What for, Charlie?"

"Don't *know*. *Did* you?"

"*No*."

"Ssh! Charlie," she cried, and I shushed.

"What is it?"

"*Them*, I think. She *is* late. Sorry you had to wait so long, Charlie."

I left the kitchen, slowly climbed the stairs.

"Who's that then?"

"Still me—*me*."

"Going to your room?"

"Yes."

"Aren't you going out then?"

I didn't answer.

"Charlie!"

I reached my room, shut myself in.

"*Char*lie."

I knew she was standing at the foot of the stairs. And I made no reply.

"Can I come up there, Charlie?"

"No, you can't."

"Why then?"

"Don't want you, don't want anybody."

"Don't you want no supper then?"

"No. I said *no*, Winifred, I *said* no," and I knew she was coming up.

"Well?"

"You think I'm queer, Charlie, don't you then?"

"I'm queer myself."

"There they are," she cried, and immediately she hurried downstairs, and went into the front room.

I heard the feet, and then the key in the door. He came in, followed by Mrs. Baines.

"S'cold in this hall, Mrs. B.," he said, but she made no comment, and I heard them go into the kitchen.

"S'nobody here," Baines said.

Winifred roared from the front room. "That you lot?"

"Is *us*, Winifred. Is Charlie in then?"

"He's upstairs."

"He's in his room, Mr. B. Spect he'll be down soon enough when he hears the supper moving."

"How long's he up there then, Winifred?"

"How do I know."

"All right, all right."

From the foot of the stairs Baines cried, "You up there, Charlie?"

"I am."

"I'll call you when it's ready."

"I shan't want any, I'm going out, Mrs. Baines."

"Bainesy, just go up there to Charlie and see what's got him. Isn't the sulks surely because we're late, go on up then."

"Charlie?"

"Who *is* that?"

"Me, Charlie, *me*."

"Why of course. Mr. Baines. Home again. Safe, I know you're glad."

"Supper's out now then," he said.

"*Again?*"

"What's that then?"

I could hear his shuffling feet on the brown linoleum.

"You never stop eating, Mr. Baines," I said.

"Sright, Charlie, work and rest, work and eat, and rest again. S'all there is."

"I shan't want any supper. I'm going out, Mr. Baines."

"Charlie?"

"Well?"

"Finished that letter then to your mother?"

"No, I haven't."

A momentary pause.

"Mr. Baines."

"Yes then?"

"You'd best go down for your meal. She'll be after you if you don't. Besides, you've been working hard all day, you'll want it, *and* that rest afterwards. Do go."

"Can I come in, Charlie?"

"What for?"

"S'just to——"

"Poor Baines," I thought, and I opened the door, *had* to. "Come in."

He stumbled in, looked shy, confused. "Do sit down. There. On my bed. What is it you want?"

"S'not going out then, Charlie," he said, and the moment he looked at me I knew I wouldn't. His eyes begged me to stay.

"Mrs. B.'s fair worried to-day, Charlie."

"*No!* I don't believe it, Mr. Baines, really," and I clapped my hand on my mouth, holding in what very much wanted to come out. "Worried?"

"S'fact, Charlie. Hard fact. Fair copped her, and me. Terrible."

I sat down beside him.

"Are you coming down then, Bainesy," and the voice of Mrs. Baines climbed even higher, "and have you told him his grub's *up?*"

"S'coming now, Mrs. B. Just coming."

"Then *hurry.*"

"Charlie?"

"Yes?"

"When Mrs. B.'s worried I just hate being on my own, s'fact."

"About what, Mr. Baines? Worried about *what?*"

"S'Lawlers really, she'll tell you, spect, trust her, Charlie, loves telling her troubles when they come. First time I ever cringed——"

"*Cringed?*"

"When he come rushing in to us, Charlie, Mr. Crawley, who else then?"

"What happened?"

"*Mr.* Baines. And get that lodger down here."

"S'coming now, Mrs. B. Right away."

"Lawlers might come a cropper, Charlie, then what? I ask you?"

"How awful. We must go down, Mr. Baines," I said, and moved towards the door. On the threshold he caught my hand, pulled me back, confided, as only Baines can. "Yes?" I asked.

"You're not going then, Charlie?"

"You mean leaving this house?"

"Sright, Charlie. Been nice having you, 'n most times I'm stuck between the two, hate it sometimes, fact," and suddenly he lowered his voice still further. "Run away twice from here, Charlie, and then come back."

"*Come* back? *Here?*"

"Well, I'm here, aren't I?"

"But why? Why didn't you stay away, and are you *never* going to be free, Mr. Baines? *Never?* Why, it's dreadful, I don't know how I stand it, I really don't—I mean——"

"What do you mean then, Charlie?" cried Mrs. Baines, dutifully waiting at the bottom of the stairs.

I pushed Baines out, and he preceded me down the stairs, and into the kitchen. The same table, and the same chairs. Baines will go to the dresser, lift up the Book, fling back the world, sit down, read from the desert. I watched him, uncertain, worried, restless, his big fingers already moving for the Book, touching it, stroking it with his thumb, and perhaps wondering, as Mrs. Baines, bent over the hob, shut off all sight of the everlasting fire.

"Do *sit*, Bainesy," she called over her shoulder, and Baines sat.

"How long's our Charlie been in then, eh?" she asked.

"Not long, Mrs. Baines," I replied. "Actually I'd meant to have a meal out this evening, and then I changed my mind."

She swung round on Baines. "No, Bainesy," she said, "not now, not at this moment, please."

"Very well," he said.

Begrudgingly he put down the Book. It was the first time he had ever had to renounce it. "Sit then," she cried, and he sat.

"Charlie's waited for hours, he's fair starving, waiting for you lot to get home," cried Winifred.

Mrs. Baines jumped to her feet. "Why, I've forgot my——" and she rushed off upstairs.

"Won't be long now, Charlie."

"He's waited and *waited* for you lot," Winifred cried.

Baines leaned over. "You starving then, Charlie. Sorry we're late, bit of overtime and a bit of trouble, s'no matter. Has *she* had hers?"

"Winifred? I don't know."

"I'll have it when I *want* to have it, Bainesy."

"All *right*."

Baines put a hand on my arm, spoke slowly, and, I thought, gave himself magisterial airs.

"Mrs. B. will be attending to you later on, Charlie."

"Thank you," I said. "I'm looking forward to that."

A whisper in my ear. "Did you have her then? *Really?*"

He rose, went to the door. "Are you coming down, Mrs. B.?"

And the next moment he, too, had departed for the upstairs region.

The hare-like ear of Winifred misses nothing.

"Gone into conference up there, Charlie, bet you, probably over ninepence. That's her all over. Everything's worked out up there."

"I thought it was," I said, "I thought it *was*."

"She'll be after you when she gets down, Charlie."

"She'll what?"

The Winifredian screech no longer surprises.

"Be *after* you. You want to see her getting after somebody sometimes, once she—can you hear me, Charlie?"

"Trying—I said *try*ing, Winifred."

Baines returned, stood in the hall, spoke to Winifred.

"You having it with us, our Winifred, or will you wait?" he asked.

"You give Charlie his tea, that's all you have to worry about."

"You are late this evening, Mr. Baines," I said.

"Hard day at Lawlers to-day," he said. "You had one?"

"Rather a funny one, Mr. Baines," I replied, and smiled.

"Oh!"

When Mrs. Baines returned she sat opposite me, but said nothing.

"Was telling Charlie we had a hard day to-day, Mrs. B."

She looked straight at me, but talked to Baines.

"Did he have a hard day too, Bainesy?"

"S'funny one, so he said, Mrs. B."

"For Charlie the world's a cushion, Bainesy. Will you serve then. That one's staying where she is, I suppose, and would do, of course, our hardest day."

Baines rose, hovered over the fire. A pan lid fell with a loud clatter, came rolling to my feet, and I bent down and picked it up, gave it to Mrs. Baines.

"Here, Bainesy," she growled, "take it. God, you are clumsy, Bainesy."

"Sorry, Mrs. B."

Mrs. Baines rose. "For heaven's sake, do sit down. I'll do it then," and she pushed Baines into his chair. And later we were actually eating again.

The circumference of life narrows, and I think of the narrowest nail, the sharpest point.

"Yes, Bainesy," she said, her eye still anchored on me, a

steadfast, yet hardly penetrating stare. "What is it then? Can always hear the words begin mumbling back of your throat." "Well then?"

"Crawley come up to me on the bench this morning, soon's I was in, Mrs. B., him early for the once, surprising really. Come up saying, 'But how in the name of hell do you imagine we're going to get this order *out*, Mr. Baines.' Always calls me mister. More'n others does."

"But we did get it out, Bainesy, we got it out."

"Terribly fussed he was, might have been angry, never seen him like it, Mrs. B. Almost the first words I heard this day was growlin' ones. Crawley just loves giving time a clout sometimes."

"He put some doubts in my mind, Mr. B."

"Oh yes. What then?"

"Doubts, Mr. B. *Said* it."

"You wouldn't think, Mrs. B., that now that Crawley's got himself hitched up again to that one from Meldey, 'n' took her to live with him at that great ugly house, Lovedene, I mean she *could* be interfering, you know that, look at her awful relations, well, look at them. If that become a hard fact at Lawlers, Mrs. B., well then, no end to the mischief."

"Mischief?"

"Mischief, in their *minds*, Mrs. B., some minds as crawls with it, *crawls*."

"With *what*, Bainesy?"

"Evil, Mrs. B. Evil. I'd be worried, that's all."

"S'true, Bainesy, you are right then. It might come to something *like* that. Ah, I'd be afraid then, Bainesy."

"Are you *really* worried, Mrs. B.?"

Shall I lower my head, shut my eyes, against this stare, unending, as she talks to Baines. And I did shut them.

"Mrs. Baines," I began.

"Course I'm worried, Bainesy, give your bit of sense a belt, will you then, for heaven's sake, course I'm worried——"

"What do you *mean* then?"

"Mrs. Baines," I repeated, "Mrs. Baines. *Please*."

"If Mr. C.'s wife does start interfering, Bainesy, then some doubts in my head will grow bigger, s'fact, dread the doubts, *dread* them. You *know* that."

"Are you asleep, Charlie?" asked Baines.

I kept my eyes closed. "Please. Ever since I arrived here, *Mrs*. Baines," I said, "I've wished to speak to you about that win——"

"What *I'd* be most afraid of, Mrs. B., would be a day arriving with an order sitting right heavy on his shoulder, 'n' him knowing then that he *couldn't* get it out, be real awful."

"It's that *win*dow, Mrs. Baines. In my *room*. I just *cannot* get it open properly, I've *tried*," my eyes still closed, my head bent, "would you——"

"Was watching that Crawley the other morning, Mr. B., caught him looking out of the window with a soft gob on him like he'd picked bluebells one Sunday in the gardens Garlan way, 'n' the world just give him a big kiss and hug. Come in with his tea, s'funny, Crawley looks different when he's sideways, Mr. B., sort of what do they call it then——"

"I know," Baines said, and perhaps didn't.

"Come straight in to him, and he didn't hear me, dreamin' there, maybe about his new happiness, copping that one on one leg, as if she ever stood on two, vain bitch, or maybe he's worried. First thought in my head was well there he is, one *we* lean on, trust and have to, Bainesy, wonder what he's thinking then as he stares and stares out of his soft mug, cup in my hand started shaking then, thinking how much most everything depended on that one, always will till the end, can't dodge nothing, Bainesy, nothing, s'fact! You *know*, just have to *trust* them, Mr. B. He heard me then, me breathing, I expect, smiled as if he didn't want to, *really*, stuttered some thanks for the tea I put in front of him, then I said, I hope it's all right, Mr. Crawley, 'n' he said, s'lovely, Mrs. Baines, thank you, sort of smarmy you might say, I went back to the door then, backwards, kept on looking at him, Bainesy, our anchor, all depending on him, all, and there he is slowly stirring the tea I give him, and some of the smile still left on him, and I thought then, 'Well, he's all right he is, so comfy there getting tea brought in to him every day of his life,' and I noticed the new suit he was wearing, *and* the tie, *yellow*, at *his* age, and I knew then, Bainesy, that the world was snug and safe under his backside—I——"

"That *win*dow," I said, "Mrs. *Baines*."

"Push it, Charlie."

"I *have*."

"Then push it *again*, ah, Bainesy, the things you can learn without ever opening your mouth, but soon's I shut that door and was gone back to my room I was thinking about this new one he's got himself, and her coming in yesterday, and catching her talking about her *shares* in Lawlers, made me worried, Bainesy, real worried, she might think you're too long in your job, Mr. B., might even ask what I'm doing there. God, Bainesy, people are terrible, terrible, can't rely on nobody these days, you can't rely——"

"All we can do, Mrs. B.," said Mr. Baines, "is hope. *And* pray."

"I suppose so."

Mrs. Baines is monumental, motionless, and her eye remains at the focal point, the lodger. Baines's hands, now resting on the table, seem to lie heavier still, almost as though the unseen Mr. Crawley had dispatched to their table a giant and invisible stone, that now lies between them, the weight of simple dread.

"What with this new fear *she's* brought into the works, Mr. B., and that one in there going off sudden like that last night, imagine it, Bainesy, in the *middle* of the night, *what* a time to feel the hunger, 'n' that's what it was, sure of it, takes them sudden, you know that, the lack never sleeps, never, horrible in a way, Bainesy, just horrible, well between one and the other I just *couldn't* sleep a wink last night. Worries me no end. No end."

"Neither could I sleep peaceful, Mrs. B."

Her eye still holds, and Mr. Crawley still remains huge.

"You can't *possibly* work harder than you do, Bainesy, you simply *can't*, and Crawley *knows* that. Silly old fool. Marrying like that. At *his* age."

"*All* the same, Mrs. B., I have a sort of feeling, a *sort* of feeling, remember what Belpin said *about* feeling, Mrs. B., well, I think he'd be fair in the long *run*, I mean——"

"There you go, trust, and trust, and *trust*, if God doesn't ever help you, Mr. Baines, I'll be real sad, *sad*. *Mean* it."

"But what more can we do then, what more?"

"How do I know?"

And dread seeps slowly into the Baines' bones. Baines turned to me.

"See how it is then, Charlie?"

"I do indeed."

"And what's all this about the window?" she asked.

"I said it——"

"Then don't say it again, Charlie. Mr. B. For heaven's sake do go up and see what's wrong with his window. Go on then," and Baines went.

"You are not very fond of the open window, Mrs. Baines," I said.

"Not all that much, thank you. Bainesy said you didn't look very strong."

"And another thing, Mrs. Baines, I've come to a decision."

She folded her arms. "So have we, Charlie."

The noise upstairs became distracting.

"What on earth are you up to, Mr. B.?"

" 'Tis stuck then, *hard*," he called down.

Her eye finds me again, holds fast. "Have *I* to come up then? You men."

"Damn!" and it was the first time I ever heard Baines swear. The next moment I was sitting alone, and Mrs. Baines was tearing upwards. The kitchen door is wide open, perhaps for my benefit. Suddenly a loud squeak from my room indicated a triumph.

"There, Bainesy, all he had to do was push, hasn't a push in him, that lot are all the same."

"It was stuck real hard, Mrs. B., Charlie's quite right."

"Rubbish! A bit of damp and no more, the fuss people make in this house, as if he was going to die for lack of air. *We* manage without it. He says he's come to a decision, Bainesy."

"Has he then? What about, Mrs. B.?"

And I had. I walked quietly into the hall, silently opened the front door, and stepped into the street. Shall I go up or down? Walk or run, and I kept looking back at the house. I felt capable enough. The grey monotones of the Baines lives fascinated yet bored me. "I shall leave to-morrow. Damn! I didn't get on with that——"

"What the hell?"

And there behind me was Baines.

"Charlie?"

"Oh, God! No," and I turned to face it. "Well?"

"Where are you going then?"

"For a walk."

"You only just got in, Charlie."

"And now I'm out again, Mr. Baines. One has to do *something*."

"How far then?" It was impossible to ignore the sudden anxiety in his voice.

"How do I know?"

"You seem angry about something then, Charlie, is it her?"

"Who?" violently, under the lamp-post.

"S'only one. Our Winifred."

I stressed and stressed, "It's *not* your Winifred."

"Who then, who?"

"I just want some quiet, some peace, Mr. Baines," I said. "I want to *think*," the words coming through my teeth, and I knew at once he was wholly indifferent, even un-noticing.

"I'm leaving to-morrow," I said. "Really going. I've made up my mind. I shall find some place in the town. Maybe my employers will help in some way. And after all, Mr. Baines, this wasn't permanent. In fact, if I may say so, it was simply in the absence of anything else."

The accusation came abruptly, boldly. "Deserting us, then, Charlie."

"I can't stand it, Mr. Baines. And what on earth's the use of my shutting my bedroom door, let alone locking it, if it *had* a lock, and how do I know the moment somebody'll barge in and wake me up? In your house nobody seems to sleep at all, perhaps they don't want to, perhaps they *can't*, but I do, Mr. Baines, I *do*. The one is always on the watch, listening for what the other will say about him. Haven't you noticed that? Does anybody ever lie *down*?"

He thought for a moment, and probably had to.

"Not really, no. Why then?"

"I wish you'd go home, Mr. Baines. Please do. I shan't be long, I promise you. And do remember what you said to me yesterday, I mean about those two being left alone together."

"Charlie!"

"What?" I asked, then suddenly walked away from him, crossed the road, and he came after me. I stood outside the brightly lit pub, studied the people going in and out.

"I'm sorry then, Charlie," he said.

"So am I. Believe me, Mr. Baines. I am."

"I mean about her, Winifred, Charlie."

My reply was casual. "Yes," I said, "of course. She is mad."

"I could tell you something, Charlie," he said.

"Please *don't*."

Baines telling me something is almost a strain on living.

"All right. I *won't* then."

I was sorry for him the moment he turned his back on me. "Tell me *what*?"

He reached up, spoke into my ear. "I once got to the end of the town, Charlie."

"Then why on earth did you come back again. To *that* house?"

"*How*? Had to, Charlie, was nowhere else, that's how it *always* is, I run off, and then there's nowhere, s'fact, Charlie."

"I'm going in here for a drink," I said. "Care to join me?"

He blanched.

"Can't."

"*Why*?"

"Just *can't*, Charlie."

"Of *course*. You see too much of Mrs. Baines. You're *not* a failure, well, not yet," I said.

"Daren't," he said.

"But *why*?"

"If they're left alone for long something'll happen, Charlie.

"Then let it happen, Mr. Baines," I cried, and I gave him a rude push and he went straight into the noisy bar-room of the Jack O' Lantern. "There!"

And he was in right against the counter, staring at me, and unable to speak. I ordered two beers. I stared round, and suddenly I saw the scoffer. He was sitting in a corner, bent over his pot. He sensed immediately that he was being stared at, and looked up, not at me, but Baines.

"Oh, God!" he cried. "Somebody's let Bainesy out."

The laughter was deafening, and when I looked round it was to see Baines hurrying through the door. I had to go after him.

"Mr. Baines," I called.

And he hurried on.

"Mr. *Baines*."

Suddenly I leaned against the wall, and laughed. I *had* to. It was quite a relief. I watched Baines get farther and farther away, then at the corner he turned round, but only for a second and rushed on. In this moment I realized the sadness of Baines. But what I didn't realize was the fact of my recognition by the horrible Scragge, who suddenly lurched out of the pub, and came staggering towards me. He stopped, looked at me, came too close, his breath stank.

"New lodger. Knew it. He had to get back then, didn't he, knew it, s'bloody house'll fall down if he don't, mister," and he laughed, which only made his leathern-looking features seem uglier still. Against my will, against every wish, I walked slowly back to the house. I knocked and waited. Knocked again. The house was silent. I tried once more. The door opened, and there was Mrs. Baines.

"Wondered where you'd got to, Charlie," she said, "'n' he just come bursting into the house like the devil was after him, 'n' he's gone out to his den, if you want him he's there. And I'll have something to say to you later, Mr. Elston."

Her tone of voice was, to say the least, brutal, the words like stones. It was the first time she had called me Mr. Elston.

"Perhaps it would be better if you said it now, Mrs. Baines."

"In *my* time, Charlie, my time," and she rushed off to the kitchen.

I visualized her return to chair and fire, and no doubt thinking hard upon the strange conduct of Mr. Baines. Alone, she may also confront that all too sudden emanation of

Mr. Crawley. I recoiled from a return to the kitchen, knew I should not go upstairs, and for a moment or two stood in the hall. I thought of Baines in his shed. I went out into the yard. The shed door was half open, and he had not lighted the lamp. Peeping in, I saw him sitting slumped in the chair. Leaning in, I called softly to him. "Mr. Baines!"

"Oh *Christ*!" he cried into the empty shed.

"Mr. Bai——" softly, and waited.

"Where then shall I go, then where?"

There was something so desolate about Baines, about the very atmosphere of this black shed, that I felt suddenly uncomfortable, remembering the too violent push I had given him, precipitating him into that too-crowded, too-bright pub.

"I'm sorry," I said.

"I know who's there," he said.

"Who?"

When he heard me come in he turned away, raised his arms high above his head, and brought them heavily to the back of the chair. He heaved upwards, then slumped again.

"Mr. Baines."

"He, he——" stuttering, "he——"

There seemed something not only desolate about Baines, but something broken, and for a moment I thought he was going to cry. I felt embarrassed, and wanted to run out. I had not quite expected this.

"I'm sorry, Mr. Baines," I said.

"What for then?" he asked, refusing to look, refusing to move.

"For what happened a few minutes ago," I said.

"S'not the first time, Charlie, s'not the first time."

"Would you like me to go away, Mr. Baines?"

He turned round to face the still-open door, but he did not look up. One hand came down to the great anchor on his knee, out of which he drew his towering trust, *now*, in the half-darkness and silence, the great hope.

"I *am* sorry."

"Once," he began, faltered, then continued, "once," and he began wringing his hands, "there was once when he," struggling again, "once——"

"Yes, Mr. Baines?"

"Scragge's come by our house one night, Charlie, s'dark, drunk he was, some others with him, stood outside our door laughing, s'always laughing out of him, could hear him, hear him talking to the others, they was drunk. 'My God,' he said, 'should've seen his *dad*,' s'my dad he meant, Charlie. 'Should've seen him,' he shouted, 'just a great bloody lump, s'all, stupid bugger if ever there was, couldn't even put one foot in front of t'other without falling over, sfact. God's kind to some of them, *sometimes*, 'n' most knows, 'n' *I* know, as how he got drawn in that time at Lawlers, s'went in with two left feet, years ago, but who'd forget that,' he said, and went on then, laughing out of him and belching, s'horrible, Charlie, horrible, Mrs. B. so shamed by it all then, 'n' Winifred sitting in the window staring out at the drunken lot like nothing was happening at all, 'n' I went upstairs out of it. *Wouldn't* go away, too drunk to move, Scragge is any time, Charlie, you don't know him 'n' I do. Was sick in the street then, s'thought he'd go off then 'n' leave us in peace, but he never did. 'S'never got any compo,' he was shouting, making the others laugh more, didn't know what they were doing, really, but *he* did, s'cruel bastard any time, *any* time. 'S'own bloody fault,' he shouted loud, telling the whole street about us, about my dad. 'S'mother was a nice woman,' he told all the world out of his drunken mouth, 'but a bit of a softy, got the Word from her did Bainesy, very warm she was on the Word,' he said, laughing again out of him like there's no end to it ever. I come downstairs then, Charlie, half-opened the front door, heard him belching again, and I didn't go out to him, and I wanted to, wanted to kill Scragge, Charlie, *kill* him, 'n' I couldn't. I cried for my will, Charlie, s'no use, just went upstairs again, that's all. S'why I run out of the Lantern then, Charlie, s'why. Might have killed Scragge, might have."

"I am sorry, Mr. Baines, really I am. Please forgive me, don't know what made me do it. Please forget it."

"I've an ache, Charlie," he said, and he raised his arms, let them fall again.

"An ache, are you ill?"

"S'in all my bones," he said.

"Mr. Baines?"

"What?"

"Did you come out here to play?"

"No, I didn't," woodenly.

"Will you?"

"No, I won't, Charlie, s'not the time for playing now. Mrs. B.'s worried no end, you saw that, count of what Crawley said to-day, so'm I. Dread the fall, Charlie, you know that."

"I do know," I said, "and I do understand," trying to find a way in.

"Do you?"

"Shall I shut the door?"

"Why?"

I didn't know, there wasn't an answer, and yet I shut it.

"Mrs. Baines told me you'd come out here."

"Did she?"

"I wish I could help in some way, Mr. Baines," I said.

"*Do* you?"

"I hope you're not still thinking about that man, Mr. Baines. I never realized you disliked him so much, and I certainly never expected him to be sitting in that pub. I——"

"Didn't you?"

"Please forget about it, Mr. Baines. I said I'm sorry. There!"

"Scragge's everywhere, Charlie, all the time. I have once——" He stopped.

"Yes, have what?"

"Forget it," he said.

"All right."

"Forget it all, Charlie."

"I'm glad."

"I give, and I give, and I give," he said.

"I know you do."

"You know what I am, Charlie, don't you? *Told* you."

"I know."

"Glad of that. Know what's on *her* mind now."

"I do."

"What she thinks about Crawley, marrying again like that, his age."

"I know that, too."

"She worries much, can't help it."

"You *all* worry, Mr. Baines."

"I'm sorry for Winifred, in *her* way, but can't say nothing."

"A pity. A great pity."

"And she's sorry too, Charlie, Winifred, I mean."

"*Winifred?* Sorry? For who? Herself?"

"For me, Charlie. S'her as told me to get off, get out of that house, run away from Mrs. B."

"I never knew that."

"Did though. So's twice I managed it, had to come back. Can't hurt, can't hurt people, Charlie, never could. Can't help what I am. *Can't.*"

"You have the Book, Mr. Baines."

"S'all I ever had, Charlie."

"You have this little place, you have your flute, you *can* play, Mr. Baines."

"Ah!" he said, and the sigh was vast.

The Baines life surrounds Baines, and, standing so close to him in the darkness, I thought of the loaded shelf below my eyes, the unread books, a world of bicycles lost between many pages, the great mystery of hydraulics, of the Self that was never quite mastered, perhaps a dream of canaries, the buried, ignored poet.

"S'people in Baptist Street, Charlie, as never looks, doesn't want to, at us I mean, call us odd, 'cause we just live our own lives according, s'minds our own business, that's what. Day *you* come here, Charlie, I said to Mrs. B., s'strange, Mrs. B. Him coming here *now*."

"Why?" I asked.

I can *just* see his hands, clasping and unclasping, hear the movement of his fingers on the paper, and that laboured breathing is strange in the darkness, something living and lost in a corner.

"S'only other lodger ever come here was Tom, 'n' he fell in love with Winifred soon's he got his head in the door, course she was loose even then, Charlie, up top. Kind of nerve jumping all the time, at anything, anyone, s'uncertain, s'moody, loving one minute, snarling next one, used to cry in her sleep before he come, and he come because Mrs. B. wanted the money *then*, Charlie, always wanting to have it, so afraid, I understand her, you see. Know all about it. S'three days here only, Charlie, in the room what you have, 'n' that Scragge knows all about it, like he'd got a telegram saying Tom'd come to us, calling out all over the street whenever he had one too much. 'Another odd'n got to number seventeen,' he says. Real scoffer is Scragge, awful creature, Charlie, half of him hanging on in any pub, 'n' other half full of teeth that's on to anything as'll feed his horrible nature, went calling out at Lawlers one day about Tom, should've heard him at it. 'S'new lodger gone to Bainesy's place,' he cries, for all the world to hear, Charlie, 'new lodger, Tom Dwile, has a mug on him as big as his backside. He'll go daft too.' That's what he said, sides all the tittle-tattle as went on after Tom died on her, s'cruel, I thought, what harm do we do anybody, what harm. World's horrible, Charlie, s'fact."

"Don't I know, Mr. Baines, don't I know."

"Winifred's mad even before *that* time, Charlie. Mrs. B. knew that, too. S'why she give in to her that time, why we go out with her Sundays to Garlan Road, what you think's cruel, but isn't really. Look in the Book, Charlie, spect you never even opened it since you was born. Mrs. B. feeds her madness, 'n' she's happy enough. Cries out for Tom in her sleep, Charlie, often. *We* know and I *told* you."

"Is there nothing you can do, Mr. Baines?"

"S'nothing really, I tried once to give her the Word, sort of balm, Charlie, soft hand on the temple, oil on the wound inside her, I used to think of the brain, ah—sort of terrible crack there, often think of it now, sad, Charlie, can't get near her, can't, no, s'our lot, is accepted by Mrs. B., by me, Charlie. S'like when Tom come, poor Tom, s'like he put a hand right inside our Winifred, lit a match, lit her up in there, s'never the same since. Can't do nothing now, nothing. Leave her be, leave her. S'another thing come to us, you know how Mrs. B. dreads the fall, Charlie, had it before, you don't know, coming from down there, know nothing. We has our worries, we'll hold them, shut the door. World's not all you think it is. Know what you think about me, *really*, about Mrs. B., about her in the parlour. No need to say anything to me, Charlie, 'n' don't feel sorry for what has come to some as may have come rightly, sort of warning, Charlie."

"I must give myself," I thought, "give."

"I understand, Mr. Baines," I said.

"I'm glad of that, Charlie," he replied.

How long will he sit here? How long shall I stand? Unconsciously, I found myself listening for the sound of the well-known voice, the call to duty. But Mrs. Baines was curiously silent. The whisper stole into the air.

"Charlie?"

"Yes, Mr. Baines?"

"I'll light the lamp," he said, and stumbled away into the darkness, groping for lamp and table.

"Won't Mrs. Baines be calling you soon?"

His reply was casual. "If she does, I'll hear. But she's fair worried, Charlie, and the mad one's always close. You know that."

He struck a match, held it high above his head, peered at me from beneath the short-lived flame. "Sit down, Charlie."

"But where will you sit?"

"S'all right," he replied, and went off to light the lamp. After which he bent down and pulled out the four great tomes on hydraulics, made a stool of them, and sat down beside me.

I searched in my pocket for a cigarette, and found none, then discovered I'd left my watch upstairs, wondered about the time. Baines took out his pipe, and I felt pleased when he lit it. I felt he had a hold on something.

"Shouldn't *really*, Charlie," he said, puffing, "s'my breathing, been told to stop, don't want to, can't."

The clouds of smoke rising, the strong aroma of the tobacco, seemed a calm on the moment.

"I shouldn't worry too much, Mr. Baines. I mean about this affair at Lawlers. After all, it may be nothing more than a rumour. Besides, I can't think Mr. Crawley could be so mean, not after your long service there, and Mrs. Baines, too, for that matter."

"The way she *dreads*, Charlie," he said.

"I know, I understand."

Suddenly he looked up at me, held me for a second with his eye, and exclaimed, "Mrs. Baines was saying to me last night, Charlie, as how almost every word out of your mouth has ointment on it."

"Fancy that," I said.

134

"Sorry you're going," he said, gave a sigh, and added, "and she'll miss the money."

"I'm sorry, too," I said.

"Everything'll be just the same when you've gone, Charlie, everything."

"I expect it will."

"Do you *have* to go, Charlie?" he said.

"I'm afraid I do have to go, Mr. Baines."

"S'pity then. I like you, Charlie. Not everybody comes out here to hear me play, s'first time anybody *ever* come when you did. I liked that. S'pity you're going then."

He paused, then continued.

"I'll be up early every morning, nails won't wait, Charlie, they never do. She'll be up, feed her bird, have our breakfast, then us off together, and Crawley'll see as we do the job proper, always popping up he is, like you might have forgot something spite of all the years we been at it, her and me. Nails, nails, nails, you just can't help dreaming about them sometimes, hammer in my head, I told you, didn't I. Sometimes Mrs. B. gets me some pills from the chemists, just throw them down the sink when she's not looking, Charlie, 'n' don't you say anything, don't you say it, will you? No. I get my calm, it comes to me from the Book. S'all as matters. I *know* you thought us odd not having any radio in this house, 'n' no newspapers now either, used to take *The Blade*, 'n' what's in it anyhow, nothing much, nothing. Have peace inside you, Charlie, that's all. Don't want nothing from out there, nothing," and he swung a big hand in the direction of the world.

His words floated away over my head. I wasn't really listening, the dimension itself is strange, and any moment now the call will come.

"It's getting late," I said.

"Is it?" so abruptly, and he gave a little jump, "what time

then?" And I wondered from which kingdom the voice had come.

"Must be after ten o'clock," I said. "I've left my watch upstairs, I'm afraid."

"Sorry to hear you didn't have a good night last night, Charlie. Mrs. B. told me, and I heard our Winifred saying something about it. But I must say you're quiet, Charlie, very quiet, *really*. S'different when Tom was here, s'breathing, Charlie, hear it all over the house, used to worry Mrs. B., but not for long, as *you* know. Told you about him going sudden like that. Strange that, Charlie, strange, a man has to wait till the day, never know when it comes, never, but it does, and s'only then you know what you are. Is some pages in the Book as makes a man shudder, but never kills you. Warns, Charlie, warns."

I got up. "I must go in now, Mr. Baines," I said.

"You *have* to then?"

"I don't *have* to, Mr. Baines," I said. "I *want* to."

"Oh!" A pause, and then, "I see. Then go then, Charlie. Just go."

"Tell me, Mr. Baines. Do you ever go in to Winifred, when she's sitting in there, so alone?"

"What for?"

"Well, to talk to her."

"Mrs. B.'d hate it, hate it, Charlie."

"Doesn't Mrs. Baines ever go in to her sister?"

"Never, Charlie. Daren't," he said.

"Daren't?"

"Sright. Hate each other, Charlie. Tried hard to get them to mend, s'no use, won't love each other any more. You saw. You know well as I do. Once, only the once I was alone with Winifred in the kitchen. Come in on her sudden. She was singing to herself, sort of humming low in her throat, 'n' smiling too, think of that, with her as never does smile really.

Never even looked at me, never said a word. And she just went on singing to herself, Charlie. 'She's happy now,' I said to myself, 'I'll leave her be,' and I left her be."

"Where did you go?"

"Upstairs," he said, and I knew it could never have been anywhere else.

"To Mrs. Baines?"

"S'right. Can't neither of us ever be out of each other's sight now, Charlie. Winifred hates her so much, if they was alone anytime for long she'd kill her."

"*Kill* her?"

"Sright. Love's dead, Charlie, that's what you don't understand. Dead. Shows you how deep he is in her, like a river, deep."

"You mean——"

"Sright. S'what I mean then, Charlie?"

"I'm surprised that Mrs. Baines hasn't yet called," I said.

"She will. In good time. She always calls."

"And you just go."

"I go."

"You spend a great deal of your time upstairs, Mr. Baines."

"Sright."

"And Mrs. Baines, too. I couldn't help noticing it, Mr. Baines."

"Sright, Charlie. Mrs. B. likes to lie, likes me to talk to her about life, I often read her the Book."

"I *see*."

"Are *you* still out *there*, Bainesy?"

"I think Mrs. Baines is calling you," I said.

"I heard."

"Are *you*——?"

"I'm coming, Mrs. B."

He rose to his feet, laboriously returned the books to the shelf, walked to the door, and looked out, glanced back at me, looked into the yard again, then quite suddenly blew out the lamp. We stood close together in the darkness, and there seemed no reason for sitting down.

"Bainesy!"

"She's calling," I said.

I felt a hand on my arm. "S'really going then, Charlie?" he asked.

"I'm afraid so," I said.

"S'pity then," he said.

"Will *you* ever go?"

"Not now. Too late. Just dream about it, Charlie, just dream."

"I dare say you'll find another lodger soon enough," I said. "Perhaps somebody like yourself, who doesn't listen or read anything except what you find in the Book. I hope you do."

"She'll be talking to you soon about last night, Charlie," he said.

"So I understand."

"Strange, her running out like that after midnight. She wouldn't even know where she was going, Charlie."

"D'you know why I took her out last night?"

"Why then?"

"I'll tell you. She came up to my room, and it's not the first time. The poor woman is all the time seeking assurance from somebody, she keeps asking me if I think she's queer. I thought a spot of fresh air might do her good, Mr. Baines. There is an appalling lack of it in the house."

"We like to keep the world outside, Charlie, you *know* that. See enough of it as it is. Mrs. B. likes to feel safe, so does Winifred. And Mrs. B. did open your window for you, Charlie, well didn't she?"

"She did."

"Well then."

"I ought to be thankful, Mr. Baines. I realize that now."

138

"Wish you'd stay, Charlie," he said.

"If only I could," I said. "There! Did you hear that?"

"I heard."

I followed him out, and as I crossed the still moonlit yard, knew that I ought to feel a little odd myself. And then the ritual of the bolts and locks and catches, the Baines fingers pawing their way towards the rightful security.

"Do you know, Mr. Baines," I said, stressing all the way, "do you know I've been trying to finish a letter to my mother for the past two days."

But Mr. Baines appeared not to have heard, perhaps not wanting to, since, at any given minute a Baines is bound to be occupied with a Baines. I heard a window slammed down. We were back, *in* the house. The great fire in the kitchen had been dampened down with tea leaves, and a cloud of greyish-black smoke filled the chimney. We stood together in front of this smouldering mass.

"I suppose that one day even *that* will go out," I remarked. He made no reply. And Baines stared, and I stared. The silence seemed unnatural. The movements above indicated that Mrs. Baines had already gone *up*. Perhaps she will see me to-morrow. I looked forward to this, intrigued by it. I thought of the silent occupant of the front room.

"What time does Winifred go to bed, Mr. Baines?"

"We never go in there, Charlie," he replied, motionless, still staring.

"Has Mrs. Baines gone to bed?"

"Not yet, Charlie. She'll be down. Wants to see you. I *told* you."

"Of course you did. Quite right. Are you going to bed?"

"Going up in a minute now, Charlie. Anything you want then?"

"*Not* a thing."

"Wish you'd stay. Such a change."

I did not reply.

Mrs. Baines called, and I thought she would. "You in then?"

"I'm in the kitchen, Mrs. B."

"Charlie there?"

"He is."

"I shan't sleep to-night, Bainesy, I know I shan't. This room's fair full of Crawley."

"Oh, *God.*"

He turned on me. "What's that, Charlie, you saying something?"

"Nothing at all."

"I didn't hear you play to-night, Bainesy."

"I know you didn't."

"What were you doing out there all that time? Talking to him about us, I suppose."

"I thought maybe you'd get used to us, Charlie, ah, I'm sorry you won't stay."

"I wonder why this town is so *full*, Mr. Baines," I said. "A pure accident I got fixed up at all."

"Progress, Charlie. Progress. Didn't you smell it then when you got here? Money, Charlie, money. And progress. The real world is on the inside."

"I hope she won't be long," I said. "I want to retire myself."

"She keeps her word," he said.

"Tell me, Mr. Baines, do you really think I took Winifred out for *that*?"

"Mrs. B. does, being a woman, Charlie. S'first time Winifred's ever been out by herself, fact. Terrible thing, Charlie, is she may have hoped. They do sometimes."

"And what do you *think*?"

Only the opening door saved Baines. Mrs. Baines came in.

"I'm going up now, Mrs. B. Good night, Charlie."

"*Go* up, Bainesy," she said.

And Baines went out. I remained standing at the fireguard, staring in. I heard Mrs. Baines crossing the kitchen. When I turned she was standing by the dresser, holding the Book in her hand. She went out and stood at the foot of the stairs.

"Bainesy?"

"Yes?"

"You'll want this to-night, Bainesy, more'n you've ever wanted it before. You remember what Mr. Belpin used to say about to-morrow, don't you? To-morrow's steps, he said. I can hear them all over this house to-night, Mr. B. Here, take it."

6

"And you just sit down there, Charlie," Mrs. Baines said.

And I sat down. Mrs. Baines sat opposite me, her arms folded, head erect, the body stiffened, the eye baleful. I could think of nothing less than a judgment. One hand gripped the fireguard.

"Did he play to you then?"

"No. He didn't."

"What was he doing out there then? Talking about us, I suppose. One of these days Bainesy'll talk his head right off. Fact."

"When I went out there I found him sitting in the dark. He had the Book on his knee."

"If he could get right inside those pages, he'd get. Poor Mr. B., I never knew anybody as so loved the Book. Do you know the Book then?"

"Not as well as Mr. Baines, or indeed yourself, Mrs. Baines."

"Thought not."

The big red hand held to the guard rail, the eye roamed my whole person.

"But I'm not wholly ignorant," I said.

"Of course not," she snapped back, "you know almost everything, don't you, Charlie? Some people are clever, I must admit that. And answers seem to come very easy to you. And you smile as easily as you laugh. Even Bainesy noticed that

as doesn't much notice anything 'cept the necessaries. Word
means nothing to you, I'm sure."

"I don't know everything, Mrs. Baines. And I never said
that I did."

I smiled, having to.

"And don't you smile at me," she said.

"*I'm* sorry."

"Bainesy's just a big baby to me, Charlie, but very obliging,
very obliging."

"I had noticed that."

"You notice everything, don't you?"

"Not always. Sometimes I'm quite unobserving."

"Fancy. D'you think I'm soft?"

"I should never say that, Mrs. Baines."

"Thank you. Much obliged, I'm sure."

"Mrs. Baines, if you wouldn't mind coming to the point,"
I said.

"You think Mr. B.'s soft then?"

"Soft?"

"And don't *smile* at me, Charlie, I don't *like* it."

She rose abruptly, crossed to the birdcage, and peeped under
the cover, perhaps to see if the parrot too was listening. She
then resumed her seat.

"I'm rather tired, Mrs. Baines, if you'd just——"

"Aren't we all?"

"*Mrs.* Baines——"

"Which brings me to another matter, Charlie," she said.

"Oh, yes?" I said, and felt some relief.

"We have a lodger here, down from London, 'shere but
two days, and then he's sneaking out of the house at half-past
one in the morning, a madwoman on his arm, taking her into
an entry no less. Did you——?"

I had to cut in rather quickly. "No. I didn't."

"Are *you* sure?"

143

"I presume you're referring to Winifred, Mrs. Baines."

"To her in the parlour."

"But she has a name, Mrs. Baines."

"Half the time she doesn't know who she is, fact. Well then?"

"I took Winifred out for a walk in the world, Mrs. Baines. As it was fast asleep there seemed little to be afraid of. I wanted some fresh air, and I hope it did *her* some good."

"*We* know what the world is, and we want none of your London lies. We all feel the lack at times. I *know* that. But with *her*, at that hour of the morning. Sneaking out, not a word to anybody. In an *entry*. Was it dark then? Was she milking the moonlight?"

"Nothing *happened*."

"God Almighty!" she exclaimed, and flung her arms into the air.

"The load on my back, load of her, load of him."

And now she was very close indeed, very intense, too close to my ear.

"Not a bin in the country'd have her, been in three, come back again, *here*. The worry of it. Ah! You don't know, Charlie, you *don't*. One mad, and the other plain soft. You know *nothing*."

She paused, but only for a moment. The eye is fixed again.

"Then you didn't——"

"I did *not*."

"Don't shout at me, Charlie."

"I'm *sorry*."

"You're angry then?"

"I'm not angry," I said. "Just surprised."

"Surprised? Why?"

"That you should even think——"

"The things one thinks sometimes, the things one has to."

Again she leaned forward, and this time I could not withdraw. She spoke so low in her throat that not even the hare-like ear of Winifred could have heard it.

"If that cage was big enough, Charlie, I'd push her into it, I would really."

"Couldn't you even *try* to love each other, Mrs. Baines?"

"Oh God! If *I* was close enough to you I could tell you the very thoughts in your head. Fact. And don't I know the thoughts in hers. My heavens! The things she *thinks, and* she's got a nice little dream locked in her teeth, Charlie. Wear me out. That's what. To wear me out. And you are sure then, about *that*?"

"I *am sure.*"

"Actually, Charlie, actually——" She paused, then continued, "I even thought, only for a moment, mind you, that you might take her away."

"Take her *away*?"

"Sright. Out of my sight. Ah, the mercy there if it'd happened, you wouldn't know the load of it."

"Good Lord! I could never do that, Mrs. Baines. Never. *Really*—I——"

"Where'd *I* find the mercy then if she come in here *now*, said you *had*? Well then? She's like that, my sister is, comes very sudden with her, *very* sudden, run out once into the night, stayed out hours, s'copper brought her back here, and the things she said'd happened, the things in her *head*?" and low, and most confiding, "If Bainesy ever looks like he's going out somewhere, even out *there*, I shudder, Charlie, shudder. Sfact. You don't know her, I do. The worry of it, the worry. I want nothing, nothing, 'cept peace. We work hard, Bainesy and me, keep her too, have to. Now he's worried no end about Crawley."

"Well, I must get off to bed, Mrs. Baines," I said.

"Course you must," she replied, and added quickly, "Course he never loved her, never."

"Who?"

"Him as lodged here, who would then. Tapped since she was twenty, he only come here account of me, that's all, 's'fact."

"And Mr. Baines? What about him?"

"He didn't mind, he never does."

She sensed my wish to be off, and herself got up, the poker in her hand, which she proceeded to drive in and out of the piled cinders.

"Mr. B. likes you, Charlie," she said.

"I'm sorry I'm leaving," I said, and got up.

"So's Bainesy. Fair sad he is. S'pity. I know what you think about us of course."

"What do I think?"

"Doesn't matter," she said, moved aside to let me pass.

"Liked playing to you out there, Charlie, told me last night."

"Nobody ever *calls* here, Mrs. Baines."

"Sright. I know."

"But why?"

"Ask her in the parlour. Sometimes she comes up in the middle of the night, wakes us up, the things she says, the *things*——"

I stood by the door, turned, looked at Mrs. Baines. "Good night," I said.

"Wait then."

I waited. She came up, put a hand on my arm.

"You won't say anything to him about what I was telling you, will you?"

"Not a word."

"Nor to that one in there."

I shook my head. "*Nothing*."

"And you are leaving then?"

"I *must*."

"And you really didn't—I mean last night——"

146

"I told you, *No*."

"Don't shout at me, Charlie."

"I'm *sorry*."

"And don't you laugh at us, either."

"I'm not *laughing*."

"And I haven't said all I wish to say," she said, placed herself in front of the door, and added, through her teeth, "not *half*."

The room, and the bed, seemed miles away, as I felt myself being pushed slowly back towards the chair.

"And you sit down there, Charlie," and I had to.

There was a call from Baines. "Are you coming up then, Mrs. B.?"

"In a minute, Bainesy. Just talking to Charlie."

"You think we're odd, don't you then? I *saw* you. Laughing at Mr. B. But he's all right, he's good enough for me, great big lump though he is. He gives me what I want, and I'm satisfied. If a woman gets what she wants she's satisfied, that's all as matters, Charlie."

"Look here, Mrs. Baines," I said, "I'm not interested, really, I must——"

"I am looking here. *You* think we're odd because we aren't rushing out into the world every five minutes. I don't know what *you* lean on, doesn't matter to me, but we lean on ourselves, thank you. *I* know what she told you. All right then. I like being flat on my back, always have. There! I'm honest. Course she thought he loved her, then why didn't she have him, why then, s'no use just dreaming about it, is it? I wanted him. I got him, what about it, what the flesh wills, the flesh *wants*, Charlie. All right. Had them before. I could take *you*, 'cept I don't want to, you're as soft as a milk pudding. Actually, we don't care who you are. I never did. Long's I have the money in my hand, it's all as matters. Just having it, Charlie, in *your hand*, got to save and save and save against what might happen, *and* it might. Load of worry on him up there now, count of Crawley marrying again, end might come any time. You don't understand nothing——"

She stood over me, tense, mountainous.

"And *she* told you we live by the Word in this house. And we do. Everything's natural to us, Charlie, everything, *and* you never answered my question, well, did you? Is what's natural good? Well then? You don't know. Of course you don't. You think we're queer because Mr. B. isn't rushing out every night, perhaps to sit on his backside in some pub and lean on what the world offers him, doesn't want it. Course he wants to get away from me, course he dreams about it, but he can't, and knows it. So does *she*, dream, I mean, like a nun now, Charlie, vowed to him out there, wreath every Sunday, thought I wouldn't *do* it, but I *did*, she was *so* surprised, the things she said to me, 'I'll break you, you bitch,' she said, 'you've killed me, you have.' Said it to me in front of Bainesy, who if he'd the pipe in his mouth *then* it would've been filled with peace, at *any* price, Charlie, that's Bainesy all over. Why, he even——"

"Will you listen to me, Mrs. Baines? *I* am *not in*terested. I——"

"But I'll wear her out, you see. I'll go out there every Sunday, wet or fine, I'll get on my knees, *to* him, *to* her, I'll show her, the things she says to me, Charlie. Surprised her, that's what I did. Crawled on my knees, *did* it. People are very strange, Charlie, *very* strange. Was a man at Lawlers come up to Bainesy one day, and he said, 'Odd, Bainesy, but I never see you in the town, don't you ever go out then,' and because Bainesy said no, he didn't much, the man thought Mr. B. was ill. Sfact. Thought he was ill, thought he was lonely even, so you *see*. He doesn't *have* to go out, and if *she* doesn't want to neither, well, whose business is it, well then? I ask you. Bainesy's right. Sright about you, Charlie. You were sad this morning, soon's he told you we hadn't the radio, and never bother about the papers much; what's in them anyway, 'cept a lot of rubbish. Some people in this world as thinks that everybody has to do what everybody else does. And just look at *her*. Isn't she odd then? I mean her in the parlour, wouldn't ever know she loved any man till it was too late. Tom was here, then why didn't she snap him up then, have him. Some people don't even know their own minds, Charlie."

"You know yours, Mrs. Baines."

"Always had to. Nothing soft down here. Tell me, is what you know too soon any worse than what you know too late, well is it?"

"There," I exclaimed, as the clock struck, and even managed to rise.

"It's very late." But she hadn't even heard, hadn't wanted to.

"Many an evening Bainesy and me sits up there and he reads to me from the Book, and a lovely reader he is, lovely. Bainesy's kind, Charlie, *kind*, works hard, expects no medals, doesn't want them. He's good enough for me while life lasts, *and* if we don't want to go out and nudge the world, we don't, *and* we're right inside ourselves, *and* nobody'll ever get in and pull us out, no, *and* we don't interfere with nobody, but live our lives according——"

"But *I* don't want to hear about all this, Mrs. Baines."

"Every house in this town is full, *and* you'll be lucky if you find anywhere, and don't count on The Gilt in Crumpton Road, people pouring into this town. That Mr. Grimpen you're going to work for, he always puts his relatives into The Gilt when they come down, which isn't often of course, probably hates the sight of them. Think of them people just pouring in, what's the meaning of it? You know, I dare say. Bainesy said to me that everything has to have a meaning for you, Charlie, is that *right*?"

I tried to rise, rose. "*Do* you mind? It's getting late."

"Look at next door, well, look at it, don't suppose you have anyhow. Knocktons, six of them, never *in*, Charlie, out all the time, *live* in the streets you might say, but it's *their* business, who minds what other people do. Other day Mrs. Knockton stopped me on my way home from Lawlers, said is anything wrong, Mrs. Baines, I said what then, 'n' she said your Winifred sitting in the window all the time, only Sundays I said, what's wrong with that, but she never goes out, she said, well what *about* it, I said. Some people can't stand not being close to you, simply hate being by themselves, that's it, Charlie, standing on the town's head, shouting all the time, that's them all over, s'what they like, *really*."

"That's enough. *Thank* you," I said, "I'm going to bed. Good *night*."

Yet I couldn't move. This kitchen was full of Mrs. Baines.

"Haven't really said half I meant to say to you. Sorry you don't like us. You won't say anything about what I've been saying, to Bainesy, or that one in there?"

"Not at all. Sorry I can't stay. I just want to go somewhere where I can *sleep*."

"We're still a bit strange to you, Charlie, that's it, isn't it then?"

"Well, I must admit, Mrs. Baines, I——"

"Don't bother to say it. When I think of the things that one thinks. And she's never been near the sea, never. What people will never do is what they most want to do. Look at him up there, look at her in the parlour. Dreams, Charlie, just dreams, only the Book has saved Bainesy from going the same road as her, sfact. And telling you she wanted to be a donkey girl at Barnton. Well, really."

For a moment I thought Mrs. Baines herself might laugh, but nothing came out, only a sudden disgust, a great disparagement.

"*Donkey* girl, Charlie. And then she keeps running up to your room asking you if you think she's mad."

And at *last*, I was *free* of the imprisoning chair, of the Baines bulk, the Baines intensity. I even got to the door.

"You won't say anything then, Charlie, about what I said?"

Her insistence was pathetic, something tragic, and something funny, menaced Mrs. Baines.

"I shall say nothing," I said.

"Thank you then," she replied, and came towards the door. I moved aside to let her pass, opened the door. For a moment only she stood on the threshold.

"Breakfast'll be in the oven, Charlie. Leave any washing out, don't turn the stove knob twice, see the doors are shut, back *and* front, don't forget the windows, and don't disturb *her*. Good night."

Suddenly, unbelievably, she was gone. It was almost a pleasure to listen again to the tumbril-like sounds as she slowly mounted the stairs. I closed the door, and returned to the fire. The clock struck ten. The movements above became heavier still. When the two Baineses move about the results sound volcanic. I looked across at the parrot's cage, the bright red cover, and thought of the bird beneath surrounded by its own mysterious silence. And then I remembered the order. I got up and went to the back door. It was already locked. I went out into the cold green hall, hesitated a moment, daring to go to the front door, soundlessly, and it, too, was securely locked and bolted. The world could *never* get in here. Darting rivulets of flame began to break through the heavy drab of the piled fire. It was almost too comfortable, too inviting to sit by. I felt I ought to go down on my own knees, pray for a peaceful night. And then I left the kitchen, bent down and removed my shoes, crept up to my room. The door was wide open. Had Mrs. Baines been in? Perhaps? Had Mr. Baines? Would Winifred wake us up? It was only after I had lain down and put out the light that I realised the window was still open, that fresh air was pouring in from the Garlston night. The sudden stillness of the next room intrigued me. Could they be asleep? Already?

"You found it, Mr. B.?"

"I have found it, Mrs. Baines."

I listened. There seemed nothing else to do.

"Then read, Mr. B."

And Joshua read:

"Into smoke shall they consume away.
The wicked borroweth, and payeth not again:
But the righteous showeth mercy, and giveth.
For such as be blessed of him shall inherit the earth;
And they that be cursed of him shall be cut off.
The steps of a good man are ordered by the Lord
And he delighteth in his way.
Though he fall, he shall not utterly be cast down.
For the Lord upholdeth him with his hand.
I have been young, and now am old;
Yet have I not seen the righteous forsaken."

"Amen," Mrs. Baines said.

A silence followed. And surely sleep will follow that.

"You were talking to him down there, Mrs. B. Heard you."

"Said a thing or two, Bainesy. He *is* leaving. Asked me where he might be able to put up, told him, lucky if he gets in anywhere."

"Very."

"He seems a bit lost to me."

"Poor Charlie. S'jaw dropped this morning, Mrs. B., when I told him we had no radio, and didn't bother about reading overmuch. So surprised he was, just as if he thought we *had* to have them things. Know what he said to me up at The Rise this morning?"

"What then?"

"Said we ought to try to live like other people—he——"

"*She* told him she wanted to be a donkey-girl at *Barnton*——"

"*No!* She *didn't*"—a pause—"*did* she?"

"Told him straight, I did. D'you know what he said to *me*?"

"What then?"

"Said to me, 'But this is all *wrong*, Mrs. Baines. People simply can't live like this to-day. They can't *be* alone any more, never again,' and *think's* said, think of what happened in the grey days, when they *were* alone. Way he looked at me, Bainesy, s'if he was God Almighty himself, said's just that you don't understand, Mrs. Baines."

"Well, *really*, Mrs. B."

"If the cat lost its tail, poor Charlie'd wear himself out trying to find the meaning of it, sfact."

"What can you expect? Look at his age, where he comes from. *Why*, just one living day at Lawlers'd rock him, rock him, Mrs. B."

"Said to him how I always took what I wanted one time, took *any*-body when I was younger, curled up with fright, Charlie did, I wanted to laugh, Bainesy, out *loud*, he's so *soft*, he thought I was going to do it on him, sfact."

Baines was slower in utterance, more thoughtful.

"Charlie's so serious about the *wrong* things, Mrs. B. Sort of obsessed, I'd say."

"I told him straight out then, Bainesy, said, 'Actually, I'm only interested in your money, Charlie, s'all.' "

"What'd he say to that then?"

"Looked too surprised to say anything, Bainesy."

"Up at Garlan Road yesterday he said to me, did I *have* to do it every Sunday, seemed surprised that some people just do what they have to."

"Move in a bit."

"I am moved in."

"I think he thinks the same as that Mrs. Knockton next door that because that one sits in the windows Sundays, it's the world's business."

"I'm not sure even yet about him, rushing her off in the middle of the night—says he didn't do anything, course they all say that, Bainesy——"

"Wanted me to walk miles with him yesterday. So surprised that I wanted to come home again."

"He just can't get over the things we have to do, Bainesy, can't. Said to me, 'Buy why d'you have to get up so *early* in the morning, Mrs. Baines. Five o'clock,' he said, way he said them words, said well then, 'We walk four miles to Lawlers,' stretched an inch then, I'm sure. 'What,' he said, 'four miles, and *back* again.' And *you*, Bainesy, you were telling him about that dream you had, all about you wanting to walk out into a long day full of snow. *I* heard, hear everything in this house, you know that."

"S'only a dream, Mrs. B. *Just* a dream. But I do give you what you want, don't I?"

"Of course, Bainesy. And glad I am of it. I love my flesh, I told him that, too; flinched Charlie did, poor Charlie, he doesn't know what's natural and what isn't, spite of all his cleverness. But you won't go, Bainesy, will you, I mean it is just a dream. I can't never help being what *I* am, Bainesy. It was a dream. You wouldn't leave me, would you, swear, oh God, swear, Mr. B. Never to leave me alone with that one, ah, the way she hates me now, hates me, never, never get out of her sight again."

"Sometimes, Mrs. B., *sometimes*, and I've told you this before, I am tired of giving, *tired*. Ah, and I'm *sick* of giving. And yet I give. I do what you want, always."

"You do, Bainesy, you do indeed. The things I told him

really shook him, Mr. B. N'the way he's always looking down his nose at us, trying to tell us he knows everything, way he *looks* at you, and so *sorry* for us, Mr. B. Sorry for *her*, too. Heard them at it. Hear everything."

"But I do give you what you want, don't I then? Peace, Mrs. B. Peace."

"And much obliged, I'm sure. Charlie's the first lodger here as ever thought us odd. Imagine that."

"Poor Charlie. Thinks the world's on the *out*side, Mrs. Baines."

"He thinks that one's mad."

"Does he then?"

"He does. He does indeed. But there's nothing very mad about the little wish inside her skull, is there then?"

"If only she'd been just a *little* like other people, like *anybody*, really, but what can you expect now, Mrs. B. I mean considering the thing you did on her. It was a sin, and think of that night, think of it, her on the brink of her bright morning, Mrs. B., and where were you? You know where she found you *then*, yes, there is always the sin——"

"He never loved her, never, *told* me, s'why he come here in the first place. Because I was here, Bainesy. *Me.* Very alive then, very alive, and ever since I married you I've been wondering—— And haven't I paid for the sin?"

"Did he have to come here at all?"

"*Who?*"

"*Charlie.*"

"Well then?"

"Everything was all right in this house till he come here, and the way he's been talking to her downstairs, heaven alone *knows* what she's been saying to him, capable of anything, the things she *thinks*, did he have to come?"

"And the room just wasting that she won't never sleep in because it's so near where I lie, and d'you think it'll last for ever, then *do* you, and that Lawlers'll put a big golden crown on your head, and say ta very much, after over forty years with them, and a little bit of gold in your pocket, Bainesy, do you *really*, and that that swine Crawley mightn't one morning tell you to put your jacket on, say go, and you start measuring the loaf again. God! Who can you rely on to-day, well *who*, *where* can you be sure, *how*, of anything, of anyone. Money's never stopped being money to me, Mr. B., and I don't care who gets into that room so long's it helps to keep off that day, dread that, dread it——"

"Don't *I*?"

"If one didn't have to trust people, Bainesy——"

"Ah! 'n' look at the world to-day that's founded on it, Mrs. B. Just look at it."

"I look. I never stop looking."

"And yet I feel sorry for her, really, Winifred, I mean. Yes, I do. Because I will now tell you something, Mrs. B. Our Winifred will die every day till her arms reach his, fact. She's like that, *de*voted to his memory. I only hope that day will be. Sometimes, I think I would die myself if Christ failed me. I do really, Mrs. Baines. Tom was so *much* to her, so big in her mind, like a whole country round her Tom was. One day you will be forgiven, Mrs. B."

"I try to do my best for all, Bainesy, you know that. Don't I guard the things that has to be, don't I do right according to you? And what's *our* lives got to do with him anyhow?"

"When I look at you Sundays, your back bent out there at Garlan Road, I know you can do no more for her, no more."

"If she'd only go, anywhere, out of my sight, Bainesy, 'n' rather her than you. Why doesn't she *try* to go out? If only she could, just the once, and by some miracle, Bainesy, find the day she wants, and the man in it. Many a time I thank God you're here, because you'll always be between us. If you walked out on me, if you——"

And the voice faltered, and finally broke.

"S'funny, Mrs. B., but all my life I only ever wanted *one* thing, to be liked, just that. Sometimes I hate this house, and yet I know it's the only place now where I'll ever be safe. Ah, I am glad of that thought, glad of it."

"You work hard, you know what you are, Bainesy, you turn up the money to me, you give me what I want. That's all that matters."

"Not all. No. I have my anchor. Him. Sometimes you've been fair cruel to me, like that time you told me I was nothing, and always would be. I was glad then that I knew there was one other, and his sad hour lives in my head for ever. We are damned, really, Mrs. Baines, and I've always known it."

"For a minute I thought it was her again, Bainesy."

"Ssh!"

Mr. Baines said loudly, "Hush."

"*I* am."

"Charlie! *Char*lie!"

I stiffened in the bed.

"Take me away out of this *bloody* house."

"There! I told you, Mr. B."

"S'dreaming, Mrs. B., just dreaming. Leave her be then, leave her be."

"*Charlie!*"

I buried my head in the clothes. When I heard the creak I knew she was coming up, *again*.

"She's not dreaming, Bainesy. She's coming up. Listen. What'll we do?"

"Nothing."

"Very well."

"Let her scream her head off. She often does that, Mrs. B. You ought to know."

And Winifred came slowly up, stair by stair.

"Take me away, Charlie, take me away from her."

"Listen, Bainesy."

"I am. Only once did I calm her down, only the once."

"Ssh!"

"They're driving me mad, Charlie," Winifred cried, "mad. Her with her money and him with God on his back. Take me away, Charlie."

"D'you suppose he did have her, Mrs. B.?"

"How would I know. You can't get anything out of him. I *asked* him."

"I wish he'd never come here, never, Mrs. Baines. There's been no peace in this house since he has. And I thought you said you were having no more lodgers after he died."

"But he's here, isn't he?"

"And now he's going, and the things he'll say about us when he does go. Doesn't think we're all mad, I hope."

"Of course not, Mr. B. He just thinks she's mad, and she is, of course. We're a bit strange to him, that's all. He's very young, he knows nowt much about life."

"Knew how to get her out though, didn't he. At that hour of the night. Must have scared her stiff, running her off like that. I shan't sleep to-night, head's like a piece of lead, Mrs. Baines, and I just can't get that Crawley off my mind. Suppose he——"

"She's still there, outside his door. Can hear her."

"Don't I *know* that?"

The short, loud laugh from Mrs. Baines was totally unexpected, and this was followed by a knock on the wall.

"*Yes?*"

"Wants you to take her out again, Charlie, for another walk. Told you she was cracked, didn't I?"

And I certainly knew who stood outside my door.

"I *won't* see her," I shouted.

"*Char*lie!"

"Why then, Charlie?" asked Mrs. Baines. "You saw her quick enough *last* night."

"I'm writing a letter to my *mother*."

"Charlie!" like a child, the finger-nails tapping on the door.

"Go to bed."

"I can't sleep."

"Neither can *I*."

"I just can't."

"*Try.*"

"I have, Charlie."

"Try again," and then I lost control. "For God's *sake*. Will you leave me *alone*?"

What followed seemed too horribly casual.

"Mr. B."

"What then?"

"Take her back, Bainesy. She calms under the Book. Take it down to her. Here. Read her to sleep."

"*Again?*"

"Afraid so, Bainesy."

"*Very* well."

"We *must* get some sleep, Mr. B. S'only since *he* come here, 's'all."

"All *right*."

The well-known thud, the door, and then the voice.

"Come then," said Baines. "Come, our Winifred, I said *come*, dear."

It was the first word of endearment I had ever heard pass his lips.

"We do *try* to love you, spite of all our worries. To-morrow, Winifred, I *said* to-morrow, I might get the sack. Think of *that*. No *work*. Load on my *head*. Please let us sleep. Just this one night. And do leave Charlie *alone*. He doesn't love you, dear, sorry, but he don't. S'just imagination. Come then."

I heard the pulling and the pushing, the struggle on the top stair.

"*She'll* kill me, I *know*."

"*Dear* Mother," and I shouted at the top of my voice, "I've been meaning to get a letter off to you ever since I got here, and only a combination of the most unusual circumstances has prevented me. However, you'll be glad to know that I arrived safely, and even managed to find lodgings just outside the town. There are any number of things I'd like to tell you, some of them rather funny, but they'll have to wait until my next letter. Meanwhile, I have taken rather a liking to the North, and I mention this especially, since I know you always had a horror of it. I——"

"He can't see you, Winifred, he won't see you. And can't you hear? He's been trying to get a letter off to his mother for the last two days. Come then. Ah, s'right. That's it. In a moment I'll give you the Word, and you'll be at peace."

The heavy, faltering footsteps in the hall, the sudden pause, and then: "Sorry to trouble you while you're writing, Charlie, but you did lock up I hope?"

"I did."

"That one's just full of fits and fancies, Charlie, you understand."

"Trying to, Mrs. Baines, *trying* to."

"Sright then, Bainesy's gone down to give her the balm. Always fixes her."

"Has he?"

"Sorry she disturbed you."

"It's all right. Please forget it, Mrs. Baines."

"Good night."

"Good night."

A shout. "Don't be too long with her, Bainesy. It's very late."

"I shan't be long," and the reply reverberated through the house.

I thought of Winifred. Was she still dressed, and blanketed, and ready for the flight. I thought of Baines, the balm. Suddenly my door blew open.

"There," Baines said, "there. *Lie*. 'right."

"I wish I was *dead*," and the voice was unmistakable.

"Lie then, quiet, sright. There! There. Listen now, just listen.

> I said I will take heed of my ways,
> That I sin not with my tongue:
> I will keep my mouth with a bridle,
> While the wicked is before me.
> I was dumb with silence, I held my peace,
>   even from good;
> And my sorrow was stirred.
> My heart was hot within me.
> Whilst I was musing the fire burned:
> Then spoke I with my tongue.

"Are you listening then, are you? Let the words come to you, our Winifred. Lie cool in you, dear. For all our sakes," Baines said.

And louder then, like a great cry through the house:

> "Lord! Make me to know mine end,
>   And the measure of my days, what it is.
>   That I may know how frail I am.
>   Behold thou hast made my days as a handbreath,
>   And mine age is as nothing before thee:
>   Verily every man at his best state is altogether vanity.
>   Surely every man walketh in a vain show;
>   Surely they are disquieted in vain;
>   He heapeth up riches and knoweth not who
>   shall gather them. . . .

"There, Winifred, sright. Easy now, s'calm."
And the voice again, out of the desert, out of the depths:

"And now, Lord, what wait I for?
My hope is in thee.
Deliver me from all my transgressions:
Make me not the reproach of the foolish.
I was dumb, I opened not my mouth,
Because thou didst it.
Remove thy stroke away from me:
I am consumed by the blow of thine hand.
When thou with rebukes doest correct man for
    iniquity, thou makest his beauty to consume
    away like a moth:
Surely every man is vanity.
Hear my prayer, O Lord, and give ear unto my cry;
Hold not thy peace at my tears; for I am a
    stranger with thee,
And a sojourner as all my fathers were.
O spare me that I may recover strength,
Before I go hence, and be no more.

"S'peace now, Winifred. Can you feel me stroking your
head? Lie now. S'cool. There! Sright then. Good night."
And I thought of the kindness of Baines. I heard him come
up, close his door.
"*Well?*"
"S'quiet now, Mrs. B. Fast asleep. Almost."
"You are good, Bainesy."
"Am I?"
"Writing a letter to his mother at this time of the night.
Did you hear him?"
"I did not."
"You——"

"I heard nothing."

"Now give me what *I* want, Bainesy."

And the just audible voice, the very words shy in their passage, the ageless surrender.

"*Very* well."

And the great creaking sound of the bed, the final blow to the day.

7

I was awake before the Baineses, and before the parrot. I lay there, inert. The prisoners were asleep, and the bars were strong. The silence seemed incredible. I talked to myself, in the absence of anything else.

"I shall leave this evening. And I must get that letter posted to-day. *Somebody* in the office will be able to fix me up, surely, prompting myself, pushing myself free from sleep, from a desire to lie down again, even temporarily. Yes, I *shall* go. Poor Baines. He'll think I've deserted him."

And then I sat up. It was very dark. I wondered about the time, and felt for the watch under my pillow. A flick from my lighter showed me that it was just turned half-past four. Suddenly, I put one foot out of bed, and then the other. I listened. I crept to the door. No lock, and no knob to turn. I opened it, and stood on the landing. I listened, and went on listening, still thinking of prisoners, of cells. Only the snores gave to the situation its proper dimension.

"Asleep! Unbelievable."

And I had to think of below, the depths, the prisoner in the parlour. Perhaps Baines is right, they are all damned. I thought of Winifred. Would she have one eye open, her ear cocked? Was Tom asleep? Inside her, crab-like, haunting, determined? I even thought of the monstrous plants. Would they smell?

In the middle of the night? And the Baines family, the great
tribe of wooden faces in black frames, staring, always staring,
at Winifred, who, once upon a time, was a nice little girl,
played on the step, hearing the man from the Insurance indulge
in the patter inherent in his vocation, the most curious traveller
working in kingdoms, on the verge of thresholds. The
pattern grows as the room grows, as Winifred lies, perhaps at
this very moment, sucked in to the same silence, and the crab
dormant, unroaming, and waiting, always waiting. I even
think of Winifred's eyelids, delicate and trembling, so finally
still under the mercy of sleep. Perhaps dreaming, perhaps not.
And if she is, then I hope the island is calm.

"Poor Winifred."

And inevitably, like a law, one must move from the one to
the other. I can see Baines, so clear in my eye, so full, so heavy
on his back in that other tight room, the dread in his bone.
And the one that is beside him, close forever. Even in sleep,
they must sentence each other to to-morrow, and to-morrow.

"Poor Mrs. Baines."

So fearful of "the fall", so conscious of trust, so loaded with
yesterday, and the day before that, the grey time, and the
fantastic climate that was neither hot nor cold, intensely relaxed, so fully grey. Her brain crowded with doors that ever
open and close, thunderous with footsteps, who perhaps sees
within the multitude her wavering and starving father, who
holds forever in her skull the very weight and sound and
sentence of that closed gate, on the day that trust died. Does
she dream, now, in the dark night? Does Crawley lie between
them, the word locked between his hands, like wind that will
blow upon dread? Mrs. Baines is sentenced to remember that
fall, on the darkest day, in the ugly town. Save, and save, and
save, Mrs. Baines. Against disaster. Baines will lean heavily
upon the Word, and Mrs. Baines will drown in her own flesh.
Winifred will feed upon Tom. I sat down on my bed, clasped

my hands, thought of my strange arrival, thought of the house first looming in an ugly library, amidst denizens in overcoats, under a Council silence. And I shall think of my no less sudden departure, perhaps into the region where things are normal, where correctness is the crutch. Perhaps behind the glazed walls of Messrs. Greele and Grimes I shall indulge in my own dreams. In my ear I can hear the sad, melancholy of Baines's *Winter Day*, and I see the great hands that know how to be gentle when clasped about a flute. I shall shut my eyes to the odd library in the shed, and I shall not laugh, obeying the injunction of Baines, respecting a basic simplicity of soul. And I sat on, in the silence, under a clock's tick, and sometimes looked towards the window that once shut out the air from a breathless man. How cool, how dark. I got up, stepped silently towards it and looked out. The world was asleep, and only mystery remained open-eyed. I wanted to move, and yet did not. Against wish and against will, I remained glued to the window, and looked out and out into the piled-up darkness. I thought of sleep broken by a strident alarm-clock, of the rising and descending, of the parrot's call, of the food that would be eaten, and of the opened door. The heavy foot of Baines stepping down into the rejected world, followed by the formidable Mrs. Baines, the feet treading into the new day. And then I turned away and started to dress.

I had a sudden desire to witness the departure of Joshua and his wife, to walk the four miles behind them, right to that gate, or door, or tunnel that would draw them into the Lawler world, that was so full of Crawley, and work, and menace. I put a shoe into each pocket and stepped out on to the landing, and again listened. The snores from the next room remained even in their rhythm. I went down, stair by precious stair, avoiding the creaks, I slid into the kitchen. And the fire blazed. Then I went out into the back kitchen and washed. The kettle that seemed always on the boil was boiling still.

I made tea, found bread and butter, and ate it. It was nearing five o'clock. I slipped out the back way, climbed the low wall, and dropped into the entry. It was quite black. I went the full length of this and finally emerged into the street. I stood hidden in a doorway and I waited for Baines. And not for long. A distant click broke the hush of the long street, and soon the heavy steps were unmistakable. I waited. Suddenly they came within the light of the lamp. Baines wore his cap, pulled tightly down over his ears, and a long blue raincoat that almost reached his ankles. I recognized the scarf. Mrs. Baines wore a long blue overcoat, the collar of which was turned up against the dank morning air. Their hands were invisible, buried in pockets. They passed by in complete silence. When they turned the corner I came out and followed them.

At this distance they took on the appearance of strange birds, as doggedly, silently, resolutely, they walked on between the huddled houses, and under the silent bridges, and crossed from one street to another, down road after road. If they had spoken into this desert of silence one would have heard them, but the words lie buried. Their shoulders seem hunched, their heads bent slightly forward, as though they carried the very weight of resolution on their stout backs. The darkness, the splashes, the very atmosphere of this sleeping town made me remember a night's fugitive excursion with Winifred, of such short duration. Suddenly they stopped, and for a moment I thought they had heard the footsteps behind them, and hurriedly dodged into a doorway. They stood in the middle of the road, looking back, a gesture of uncertainty, as though something forgotten had been suddenly remembered. Then Baines moved, and I saw he was taking out his watch. Too early? But never too late. He looked up as if expecting rain, turned sharply on his heel and went on, followed by Mrs. Baines. It was now half-past five.

"Probably start work at six o'clock," I told myself. Rather early. But perhaps Lawlers was like that, perhaps Crawley himself liked to have an edge on the world, to be always a little ahead of the clock. And at this moment Baines seemed hardly a will-less man. There was iron in his walk, in hers, a determination, a devotion to duty. They looked neither right nor left, and heard nothing save the sound of their own footsteps.

Suddenly we were in another part of the town, and one that I had not seen. The houses had vanished. There were only factories, high and low buildings, of iron, of stout stone, of wood, of corrugated iron. And chimneys, and more chimneys, pushing skywards. The lamps seemed more numerous here. Strange shadows reached out to each other from either side, like enormous hands, elongated heads. I wondered if the Baineses noticed the Baines shadows, so well ahead of them, and ten-foot long on a smashed and torn, and pitted road. Somewhere in the distance a hissing noise, and, as we drew nearer, it increased in force, as if some hidden engine had reached its peak of effort, and might now explode. And clanking sounds, and sounds of metal, and glass, and tin, and creaking wood. In the middle distance, and somewhere to my right, a gaunt crane, and beyond it a faint russet glow in the sky. The Baines pair went on, turned sharply right, and crossed a low wooden bridge. When they reached the other side they stopped, and I knew they had reached Lawlers. The world of nails.

Suddenly a man emerged from a dark doorway, was caught by the light, was surprised by it, as though he had never before seen a lamp, looked up at it, and then exclaimed loudly enough for the area to hear, "Christ! When does it end then, then when does it end," and soon vanished into another doorway. I was so fascinated by the appearance of this man that for a moment I lost sight of Baines, and when I saw them again they were passing through an open gate that gave on to a big concrete yard, down one side of which stood a number of wooden sheds. In the farthest one I noticed a light in the window, the man beneath it, seated at a small desk. Towards this the Baines pair now walked. The window shot up, there was a quick exchange, and the next moment they had vanished behind the sheds. Should I wait to hear the sound that reached from this shed to Baptist Street, to Baines's bed, and ended up in his head? The journey was over and I did not wait, and turning on my heel went back the way I had come. Soon I heard footsteps, then voices. I knew that Baines was always first at Lawlers, and would never be the last. Crossing the wooden bridge I heard voices that were closer, high and shrill on the morning air. The figures of two young women approached me, there was a burst of laughter. Rain-coated against an everlasting climate, they wore bright squares on their heads. They did not even notice me, but as they passed I sucked in the words like a sponge.

"She's expecting a baby Saturday."

"Who then?"

"*Elsie*. I told you."

"Oh! What colour?"

"Never asked."

And then they were gone. Down the pitted road, past the towering pile of barrels, the empty crates, and the rubbish dump that may have lain there since the beginning of time. I thought of Baines bent to his nails, and of Mrs. Baines being almost *everything* at Lawlers. And I was bound to think of Winifred. Would she be up? Huddled to the kitchen fire, now that those others had gone out, filching the warmth? Should I go back to the house? Or should I roam about this town until it was time to go behind the glazed bricks of the offices that would always look like a pub? I made up my mind, walked slowly towards Baptist Street. Perhaps at this time of the morning other kinds of life might emerge from it. I pushed myself forward with words.

"I shall leave this evening."

A convoy of lorries tore past, their lights hooded. A group of men ambled past, and certainly seemed in no hurry to meet the day that was waiting them. I turned the corner and found myself in the longest road. At a fixed point Baptist Street will split it in two. Perhaps it is only the quality of the light, but suddenly the shops I pass appear sequacious. A thousand doors seemed opening and closing. Garlston was waking up. Alarm-clocks split the air into fragments. Footsteps rang out everywhere. Men passed me by, singly, in groups, one such very close together in conspiratorial whispers about something that was probably important. And the first cyclist, and one more raincoat. The morning patterned a forest of shadows. One passed through chambers of light and darkness. And then I reached the pub into which I had so rudely pushed Baines. Its maroon and white walls seemed more brilliant still under the light of the lamp, and had it shone brighter might have revealed the shoulder rubs of half the town. On the opposite corner three men stood waiting for the bus, whose distant screeching of brakes could be clearly heard. Then suddenly it was in view. Bright orange, it serpented the corner like flame. A near-by clock struck seven. How many nails had Baines hammered in? Had Crawley arrived? Was Winifred still asleep? Would Mr. Greele be of any help in a very pressing situation? "I must find a place by this evening. I just can't stay there any longer."

The keeper of law and order passed by, his vigil over, and the blue light over a doorway beckoned him home.

"And I must post that letter to-day."

And there was Baptist Street. And there was the entry where darkness is total. Behind the high wall that hides the junction I could already hear the cries of men, through cupped hands and through megaphones, a distant sound of shunting. And later the roar of an express train.

"I must get my things together."

A silence is momentary, and then is broken by a great hiss of steam from a stabled engine. Suddenly I was glad I had brought my torch. I shone this into the long corridor, and the light met a line of small wooden doors, each one of which seemed to be painted in a different colour. So slowly down, groping through the darkness, the damp, and seeing at the far end the single pinhead of council light.

"No use knocking at the front door. It won't be opened."

Past a pink door, and then a yellow one.

"The Colour Council would simply love this," I thought.

"Here we are," and there I was, right outside the Baineses' back door, and still hesitant.

"I could go *now*."

The lights came on from window to window, and there seemed no end to the strident alarm-clocks. It made me look up, think of my own room. The lock that wouldn't lock, the monstrous wardrobe in which lay my things. The window that was still miraculously open. Perhaps next week it would be nailed down again. The iron bed in which I tried to sleep. Whenever I looked up the angel in flames was always staring down. And then I remembered the letter lying on the table.

"I *must* post it to-day."

I knew the back door was locked, and yet I tried the catch.

"Poor Baines. I'm beginning to think he did like me in his curious way," and I could only think of him sitting alone in that shed, playing to himself. A fusillade of banging doors, and then the sound of many feet.

"I'll settle up with them this evening. Leave in the morning."

And then I climbed the wall, and dropped into the yard. It

was with a certain dread that I put my hand on the latch. Suppose it, too, was locked. I hadn't even shaved. No. Open. I went inside, stood a moment, listening intensely, out of sheer habit. Soundless. I opened the inner door. The fire met me with a dull roar as some coal collapsed and burst into flames. If this furnace should ever die out the house will never be the same again. The remains of the Baineses' meal covered the table. I was glad to sit down. I lit a cigarette, proceeded to stare up the chimney. When I glanced at my watch it was twenty minutes past seven.

"Might as well go up," I thought.

Something made me turn and look at the cage. The cover had been removed, and the bird was staring at me. I stared it back, and its head suddenly dropped. I removed my shoes and left the kitchen. I listened again. Not a sound. I went slowly upstairs. The Baineses' bedroom door was partly open, and I had a quick glimpse at clothes scattered about the floor, presumably a hurried departure. Were the Baineses late, for once? Something made me peep behind this door. The Baineses' bedclothes seemed irretrievably twisted, and a wardrobe no less ugly than my own stood with its doors swinging open, and its contents in utter disarray. In one corner, looking *very* personal, a pair of Baines's heavy black boots. It brought Mrs. Baines to mind at once, and I could see her hovering over Baines with her everlasting complaint, "And don't *clump*, Bainesy, the clumping that goes on in this house, the *noise* you make just going from here to there."

The room looked like a battlefield. Had they quarrelled? Fought each other? For what reason? Or was their very departure in itself desperate? Had they wanted to rush out very suddenly, from their own horror? The window is as small as my own, is closed, and draped with a green curtain. Under it a chair, and on the chair the Book. There was no fireplace. On the wall above the bed a large photograph, in which six men with folded arms stared resolutely ahead, and at their feet a neat pile of wooden balls. The bowling team. The younger Baines on the right, huge, even at that tender age. Looking more closely I knew it was Baines being twenty. Was it possible? Had he actually had a youthhood? Of Mrs. Baines's earlier years there existed no trace. Not a book in the place, not even a copy of *The Church Gazette*. The linoleum glistened, and it wasn't green. In another corner there lay a pair of Mrs. Baines's shoes, of a loud brown, and heavily worn down at the heels, evidence enough of her daily marathon to the nail factory. No vase, and no flowers. Beyond the window, more bricks, more slate. A room of the hooded and secret life. At what precise moment, on what day, had this strange pair first registered their disgust of the world? And the bed. Giant, half filling the room, the clothes tossed, one pillow half over the edge. As strong as a battleship, with its four shining brass knobs, over one of which was draped a shawl, over the other a shirt. This was where Baines heard the sound of the hammering, where Mrs. Baines worried, and dreaded the fall. Where Baines read the Book, and Mrs. Baines listened. The wallpaper was of a vivid red on which grew flowers of many colours. It seemed like a gesture to the whole room. I wondered who had chosen it. I looked at the bed again. Perhaps Winifred would make it before their return, her fingernails tearing at the sheets, her violent, nerve-ridden hands thumping on the pillows. I almost felt her behind me, her breath hot on my ear, intensely confiding. "S'where they lie, Charlie. S'where they argue about the money."

I tried to think of a word that would match the room. It posed a question, and there wasn't an answer. I turned away and went into my own room. The window was still open, and a sudden gust of wind set my door banging. I shut the window and sat down. The moment I set eyes on my suitcase the monstrous wardrobe seemed beckoning. I got up and opened the top drawer, and took out the letter.

"This I *shall* post to-day."

I read it, then folded it and put it in an envelope, sealed it, put it in my pocket. "I ought to get out now, this very minute," and knew I would not. I thought of Baines arriving home, bursting into the kitchen, seemed to hear him exclaiming, "S'Charlie gone then." Poor Baines. I must say goodbye to him. I *can't* run away like this. I wonder how he got on to-day. Did Crawley——"

The window blew open the door. When I got up to shut it I knew it was too late. Winifred was standing outside the door. There was a strange smile upon her face, and her hands were loosely clasped in front of her.

"Good morning," I said, rather stiffly, though civil enough.

"I heard you going out," she said, leaned against the door. And I had to answer.

"Did you?"

"Yes."

I put my heel to the door, ready to kick it shut.

"I'm just gathering my things together," I said, even smiled back, and added, "I know you'll excuse me for a few minutes."

"Sorlright, Charlie. I know."

I decided not to ask her what she knew.

"You went out for a walk, Charlie."

"That's right. I woke rather early, and couldn't settle down again."

"They're worried no end."

"I *know* that."

"Should've heard them at it."

"I did. I thought it would *never* end," I said.

I turned my back on her, picked up my suitcase, and proceeded to throw one thing after another into it. I shut the drawer.

"That was last night, Charlie, s'morning I mean."

"Not *again?*"

"Sright. They were at it, Charlie, heard them, she thinks Bainesy'll get the hook any day now count of Crawley marrying that one. Be awful, Bainesy once had to go on the Public, she hates *that*."

"I know that, too."

"You do know a lot, Charlie, don't you."

"I know practically nothing," I said, "I'm learning."

"S'wonder they haven't sacked Bainesy long ago, Charlie, he's so soft."

"I like Mr. Baines," I said.

"Know you do. What about it then?"

"Nothing at all."

"S'whole life's been spent there hammering in Lawlers' bloody nails, Charlie. There's a chap there as works by Bainesy name of Scragge, know him?"

"No. I don't know him."

"Laughs his head off at Bainesy, only cos he's so soft, s'all."

"I'm not interested."

"Know what she said to him last night, Charlie?"

"I don't care what she said to him, or he to her, and I'm not really listening to what you're saying."

"Said I wish to God he'd take her out of my sight, Bainesy, we'd be on our own then, and Mr. B. said she hadn't got to be so silly, s'only nineteen. Are you only nineteen, Charlie?"

"*I* am."

"I'm forty-six," Winifred said.

"*Are* you?"

"Be terrible if he gets hooked, she'll cry and cry, way she does carry on."

"Nothing can be worse than it is," I said, and I shut the door in her face.

"Call you when it's ready," she cried, and went off laughing.

"Poor creature," I thought.

The door below *banged*, as usual.

Shall I be sorry for her? Until the end?

"S'ready now, Charlie."

"I've had my breakfast," I said.

I dropped everything and went to the door. "*Had* it, Winifred."

"Know what he said before he went out."

A door is no barrier to Winifred, and distance no object. A thought in Winifred's brain *has* to escape, at any moment, anywhere. Her thoughts lie, restless, unaccountable, waiting, and not always for the spur of the moment.

"Said he likes you being here, Charlie."

Poor Baines. With his trust, and the things he clings to, even the slightest thread.

"Did he, *really*?"

"S'ready now."

"I must shave. *Shave*," and the words followed my feet. I passed through to the back part of the house. I began to shave.

"Can I come in?"

"If you want to."

"I'm sorry you're going, Charlie."

"I shan't be a tick," I called out, and then I heard her moving towards the table, a big chair being pulled up, a violent clearing of everything, and then the shout.

"Out."

My last day in this house. Whom shall I thank?

She was herself seated, a cup of tea in front of her.

"S'there."

"Aren't you having anything, Winifred?"

"Cup of tea, s'all. Never eat much really."

The egg was hard, the tea thick, sweetish.

"I shall be leaving in the morning," I said.

"I expect you will."

"I'm sorry for Mr. Baines."

"I know."

"I'll often think of you, wonder how things are getting on, what you're doing."

"I'll just be going on, Charlie, s'usual, living, I suppose."

"I suppose so."

"*Char*lie!"

"And Mr.——"

"Oh, *him*. He'll just go on not minding, s'him all over, Charlie. But I'll break her, I *will*. Poor Bainesy, never slept a wink last night, works so hard he does. Told him twice to run off, he *can't*, and he knows it.

"Funny dream I had last night, Charlie. I was——"

"Dream? I didn't know you were asleep. I thought you were listening to the row upstairs?"

"Dropped off sudden."

"Oh! I *see*."

"You didn't tell me a lie, then did you? That night?"

I sat up at once. "A lie? When? What night?"

"Night I come in to you, and you shouted at me, you did, you *know* you did," her voice broke, "you told me to get *out*."

"I'm sorry. I told you then, didn't I?"

"I'm not mad, really, am I, Charlie?"

"Of course you're not. I told you that, too. Remember?"

In a moment a cup and saucer smashed, the cloth was dragged against the weight of her body, and her arms shot into the air.

"Sometimes I wish to *Christ* somebody'd like me, Charlie, I do."

Her face disappeared behind the back of her hands, and the tense fingers seemed to drive into the skin. The next minute her head was flat on the table.

"I meant what I said, Winifred."

I drew back from the table, a cup and saucer in my hand, and watched her own clutch at the cloth. Her arms were stretched right across the table. It was as though somebody had struck her a sudden blow.

"Winifred."

Slowly her head came up, the eyes opened, looked at me.

"I'm not mad, am I?"

I shook my head.

"*Sure?*"

"*Sure.*"

"Want more tea then?"

"I should love another cup. Thanks."

"When you're gone I'll be here, and when they come home in the evening I'll be here, and when they come down in the morning I'll be here, Charlie."

"You said you were dreaming."

"Sright. Was a long tunnel and I'm in it, Charlie, s'lights *all* the way, and little doors, tiny, s'like a tale I read once when I was little, s'a hand in the air, a little finger moving, s'like it's talking, come on, it says, come on then, so I was coming on then, up the tunnel and the lights shining, on my face, Charlie, s'funny then something happened." She stopped dead, closed her eyes, opened them again, looked at me, beyond me, stared round and round this kitchen.

"What was funny?"

"S'hand vanished, then gone, doors opened, s'a hand sticking out of each door, s'hand's a face then, smiling at me, Charlie, s'heads moving, I went on down past the doors and then they shut——"

"How very strange——"

"S'hand in the air *again*, waving me, I waved back, s'a man then, smiling, then just a mouth, Charlie, it said come on and I come on."

"What happened?"

178

"S'walking to the end of this tunnel and there's the door, open, all the day outside, I could see the sun, s'fact, shining out there, I'm turning my head, then looking back, and s'nothing back there at all and then I saw him. He was there. I wanted to shout and I couldn't, wanted to scream, s'a hand come over my mouth then, and——"

"*Who* was there?"

"Bainesy," she shouted, bereft, a terrible momentum.

"*Mr*. Baines?"

"S'on his face, flat, Charlie, 'n' she's standing on him."

"*Who?*"

"*Her.*"

The harsh voice, the hate in the word, I can only think of the trance-like morning at Garlan Road.

"Be normal," I thought. "Nothing is odd."

"How extraordinary, Winifred," I said, trying to be casual, determined to remember the night before, and the night before that, in the area of dementia. Suddenly she was upright in her chair, the head slightly fallen, and then the drumming upon the table, suddenly uncontrollable.

"Her face was to the wall, Charlie."

"Yes?"

"S'hands clawing on the floor, s'pages and pages blowing everywhere, everywhere, Charlie, all down the tunnel, 'n' out into the air, blowing and blowing all over the place, s'his Book, I knew. *Saw* it. S'all *over* the tunnel, doors opening again, s'hands coming out *again*, s'little ones, big ones, all grabbing at the pages, s'him on his face, *was* him, I was bending down then, Charlie, looking at him, saw one eye then, s'open, staring at that wall, saw her big feet on his back, s'not moving at all, not an inch, *very* still then, poor Bainesy, s'very still, couldn't see her face at all then, s'right against the wall, she was pressing on him, could almost *hear* her pressing, Charlie, s'fact, s'a man then, sudden, at the door where the light was, tall, oh *very*, hands waving at me *again*, then him saying come on, come *on*, likes desperate wanting to get hold of me, pull me out where the sun's shining and the papers blowing *all* over the place, *she* had her big coat on half over her head, one she wears only *sometimes*, her best, covered her all over, s'first time I ever saw Bainesy without his boots, s'fact, just his socks, he was close to the wall like her. I bent down *again*, Charlie, *saw* it then——"

"Saw *what*?"

"The Book, Charlie. *His*. The big one. S'in tatters. I nearly cried looking at it."

"What a strange dream, *very* strange," I said.

"Woke up, then, very sudden, and it was her, at him again, up there, told you I heard what was going on up there last night, way she gets after him all the while. You heard it, you *know* you did."

"I really ought to be on my way," I said, "it's rather late."

"If that one could only find a Lawlers' nail long enough she'd nail him to the house so's he'll never get anywhere, Charlie, s'fact. She's like that, my sister is, always was, always will be; she knows I'll never let her alone for it, never."

The witch is back in the kitchen, and Winifred is riding her, round and round.

"It's a wonder the people next door don't complain, Winifred. I mean about this talking that goes on every night, it never stops."

She was calm in a moment. "S'Foulkes you mean, Charlie."

"That's right."

"S'telly on there every night, and the gramophone going up top, and there'll be five of them in the parlour any time, and some people as comes in sometimes, and there they are, Charlie, all talking at once, s'never hear themselves hardly, never mind anybody else, so's never hear *her* getting after Bainesy way she does sometimes."

"I think it's a great pity, I really do."

"S'all worry, Charlie, where'll they end up, where, that's it, *all* the time, s'nothing for them anywhere, *really*, s'if Crawley cracks down on him, old bastard, knew a girl there once as used to work for him, s'married *again* now, they say, I hear things sometimes, course you wouldn't understand anything about *that*, don't have to, you're you, and he's him, and she's her, never understand, never. Even Bainesy's odd sometimes, Charlie. S'a day he was sitting by that window, he did look grey that time, head half out, sort of sad-looking he was and she come bustling in then 'n' soon's she saw him she was shouting into his ear-hole, 'Are you listening for the big trumpet, Bainesy——' "

"It's getting late," I said.

"I expect it is. You do understand, Charlie?"

"I am *trying* to."

"Are you?"

"Yes. I *am*."

"If you'd only *seen* him, oh God, I can't get him out of my head."

"But it was all right in the end, wasn't it? It *was* only a dream, and you woke up, and it was all right, Winifred, he was up there, in his room, he was safe enough."

"She was getting at him."

I had to drag the words out. "You told me that already."

"Did I then? Sorry, Charlie."

"*No* need to apologise."

When I rose she rose, when I walked to the door she followed me, when I entered the hall she was behind me; I wondered if she would follow me upstairs. But she stopped suddenly, and said, "You *are* leaving then?"

"I told you. In the morning."

"Sright. You did. Sorry, Charlie, I just forgot, s'all. Sometimes I do forget things. Going into my room now."

"*Do.*"

I watched her turn, this tall, thin, tormented figure, hunch-shouldered, and I thought how only the thin back supported the total, her masthead. She glanced down the hall, then went quietly to her room.

"I wonder what she'll see when she looks out of the window this morning."

I hoped it would be something nice, even something new. Such a change for Winifred. And five minutes later I was out, clear of the cells, the fug. And the air outside, the space. It was wonderful. I had to proceed down Winifred's "jowler" for the sixth time, since Baines is always so careful to lock the front door. Strong smells of detergent, stale food, but not a soul in sight on the long passage which eventually took me out to the top of Baptist Street, which I still think is the longest in the whole town. And fortunately for me one of those flame-coloured buses just coming round the corner. It was crowded, mostly with women, and they seemed entirely in agreement about something that had happened in Garlston only yesterday. They concentrated on this, talking at the tops of their voices. I didn't even listen, I had done so much. Besides I found the bizarre colouring of the bus so attractive, a brave break into the mass of grey and black and slate of which this tight town appeared to be made up. And the women went on talking, excitedly, and the conductor, gruff but kindly, gave everyone a ticket. I was looking forward to arriving in a normal area, and he was obliging enough to see that I got off at the right corner.

"Much obliged."

"S'O.K.," he said in between his teeth.

Down Pelops Street and into Stavanger Road, across this and into Castle Place (no Castle in sight) and there lay my destination. Like a vast father, a policeman shepherded many children across the traffic-torn road. I could see the bold brass plates on the wall, the names shining in the morning light. Greele and Grimes. The glazed white brick, the big black door. It was five minutes to nine. I entered and made for Henge's office. The first thing I heard was my own name.

"Came down here Friday, I understand, young chap, says he wanted to get as far away as possible from his mother. He——"

"They all do. What's he like?"

"None too bad. Only saw him the once, after old Greele had given him a going over. Seemed somewhat surprised at the large population here, and almost angry because he couldn't get fixed up the moment he arrived."

"They expect the earth."

"Only decent hotel in the place was packed, but he managed to find some place out of the town."

"Silly ass. Why didn't he book in normally."

"I think he did, but somebody forgot all about him. He's a good way out. Anyhow, you'll see him soon. Has Grimes come yet?"

"Not yet."

"What's his name?"

"Elston. Charlie Elston. Around twenty I'd say, not bad looking. Just fancy anybody coming from down there to work in this hole."

"Somebody coming."

It was me.

"Good morning," I said.

"Hello," they said, as with one voice.

I entered and shut the door.

"You look tired, Charlie. It is Charlie, isn't it?"

"Do I? Yes, it is Charlie."

"Got fixed up all right?"

"Yes, thanks."

"Seen Grimes yet?"

"Only Greele."

"God! Wait till you see him. Last one out of that hole, famous one——"

"Calcutta."

"What's it. How'd you like old Greele?"

"I didn't find him too bad, I had expected worse."

"You're a good way out."

"Yes."

"Everything O.K.?"

"Not quite."

"Henge was just saying to me how surprised he was anybody'd want to come to work in a place like this. Seems odd, even to me."

I smiled. "I'm a bit odd myself."

"*Are* you?"

"You haven't met Dick?"

"How do you do."

Dick is one more blue suit, a real buzz of fair hair at the top, and sharp, shining black shoes at the other end. Pimples congregate when he smiles. He is grey with a clerk's paleness. He swung himself round and round on the swivel stool. The chin rests on the bright bow, yellow spotted. Henge is taller by a head, almost smells of navy, turkey red countenance, on the hairy side. He was dressed in sober grey. The collar was immaculate, the tie bootlace thin. He gave me the impression that he would sit carefully in any seat. He is above Dick, and I'm below them both. I was handsealed, unproven, and groping. I sat down on the only vacant chair.

"Think you'll stick out the full time here, Charlie?"

"Why not?"

"What's your line when you're not being busy at the very bottom, and wondering what day you'll reach the top?" Dick enquired.

"Walking mostly, some reading, musical too, all kinds."

Henge pulled out a gold watch from his vest pocket. Nothing on the wrist for Henge.

"And you'd best get going," he said, and Dick ceased circulation at once, jumped off the stool, and rushed out of the office.

"Nice chap, Charlie. It is Charlie. Charlie Elston."

"That's right."

"Are you all right?" he said suddenly.

"All *right?*"

"You look a bit under the weather, sense of strain, you look tired, Charlie."

"You said that already," I replied.

"Ah well! You're the gentleman of leisure until you've seen old Grimes. But you'll be here, and I'll be giving you the one-two, one——"

"Thanks."

"But quite seriously, you are all right," and Henge's eye was roaming, trying to find a way in.

"I've never seen such a crowded town," I said.

"It is pretty crowded, and they seem to be coming in all the time. Sometimes I ask myself when this crowding-in business will cease."

"I noticed that as soon as I arrived. It was only by a stroke of good luck that I got fixed up at all."

"What kind of show then?"

"Working people. Quite respectable, rather talkative, a tiny house, meet yourself everywhere sort of thing, but better than nothing."

"Anything's better than nothing."

"It is."

"The next town's even *worse*. Here there's room for every-body, I mean at the top and the bottom, and in the middle. Traffic's all one way at Grayley."

"Is it?"

"See that chap there," Henge said.

"Which chap?"

"Behind you. Staring in here. Always likes to stare in. You'll get used to him. Probably feels lonely if he's out of reach of anything on two legs. In a way, *queer*."

It was only when Henge waved that I turned round, and there was the tallest man I have ever seen, an expression of the utmost concern upon his face, a long face, lantern-jawed, almost choked by a stiff collar, and some grey hair anchored right in the middle of his forehead like a third eyebrow. He stared at Henge, at me. "Ledger clerk here for ages, Charlie. Decent enough chap, as they go."

"I'm sure he is," and I waved too, and, gravely, he waved back. Then he vanished.

"You talk about overcrowding, Charlie," said Henge, "well, that chap there now, take him, Roley's his name, lives out Top Bank way, married, three kids, he went away on holiday last year, Lakes, I think, and when he came back two weeks later he was just able to get inside his own home. There were five more in the house when he got back. His sister's husband and three kids. It's the way it goes, this transferring people all over the place, moment's notice, no more, get where you *got* to get, *get* there, another new branch for somebody, another plastic factory, Charlie, full of busy people turning out millions of things made of more plastic, a bit mad the whole thing. *And* they keep on coming in, God knows what for. Isn't the detergents, and *that's* stinking everybody out, perhaps it's some particular quality in the Garlston mud. You never know, do you."

"You never know. Will Grimes be long?"

"Turns up tennish, *very* posh, big car, water bottles all over the place, naturally he's a bit fragile. Lives inside his umbrella you might say. Testy. Stuffed with correctness, *stuffed*, and tradition, and decency, and loyalty, almost all the old-fashioned things."

"Sounds interesting," I said.

"How about us getting together this evening, Charlie?"

I was prompt enough. "Can I think about it?"

"Of course. Do. *Think*. But be careful, never know what *I* am. Never know what anybody is to-day, do you? Well, look at people, *anybody*, ah—there's something now."

And it was. The car. The fragile man. The engine purred outside.

"He'll ring for you."

"Right."

"Married?"

"Me? No. Are you?"

He sniggered. "Butlerian line for me, chum, cheaper to buy the milk, etc., etc."

"I see."

"Glad you do. You still look rather done in to me though."

"Haven't slept very well," I said.

"New place, new atmosphere, that's it, I expect."

"I expect it is."

I will be glad when Grimes rings, Henge might talk his head right off.

"Well, if you do feel like a bit of social stuff, Charlie, just give us the signal. Might go over to The Boot Box."

"The Boot Box?"

I must have sounded somewhat incredulous.

"Pub," he said.

"I'll see."

"There she goes," he cried, and there she *was*, going, something like a cracked bell reverberated through the corridors.

"Mr. Elston?"

And when I turned round there was a girl with a doll's prettiness and a hair style that was right on the dot.

"Mr. Grimes wishes to see you," she said.

I followed her down the corridor, she threw open a door, and announced my name. The door closed behind me. A big room, a big desk, a little man. Shelves groaning with tomes, right down to the thick carpet of brightest red. A tiny voice.

"Mr. Elston."

8

JUDGEMENT DAY

I imagine Winifred is dead. In the parlour. Worn out, at long last. From waiting, from watching. Silence makes me think of the Dead Sea, a calm lake, a mountain of stone. Had *he* perhaps come? Seen her sitting in the window, wide-eyed, mute? Faced her, at last? Rushed in, pressed hard, got her? Are the claws loosened, have the doors refused to bang when closed? Has he dragged her out there, drowned her under the flowers? Is she now beyond flesh? And did she cry, *Tom*, before the mouth fell, heavily hung? Are they happy now, forever and forever? I looked up at the angel, restless in flames. Does she hear the sea flow at Barnton, the donkeys galloping in heaven? Where now, at the end of a long day, can she cry, "*Bitch!*" I shut my eyes, against a ceiling that is low, flaking, dark-stained. Against the pull of Baines land I thought about Henge. About a world with Greele in it, Grimes, and Henge. "Thank you, Henge." Because I had had enough I hit him with words. I was faster than the parrot.

"Anywhere," I said. "Anything."

And the moment I heard myself say it, Henge was real.

"You sound quite desperate, Charlie," he said.

"I haven't slept for three nights."

"Good God!"

"They never go out."

"Who never goes out?"

"One of them is trying to raise a man from the dead——"

"Are *you* all right, Charlie?"

"Am I all right? I love that. I really do," and I laughed then.

"Hold on a minute, chum, hold on."

"And they dread the fall——"

"Now look here, Charlie—*really*——"

"He had a wooden head, really wood, he told me himself——"

"Charlie! Do pull yourself together."

"Have you been to Garlan Road?"

"No, I haven't been to Garlan Road."

"The wreathes are six-foot high."

"You're drunk."

"I'm not."

"You are, you bloody well *are*, Charlie."

"I am glad of that."

"Glad of what?"

"*Nothing.*"

"You're ill."

"Am I?"

"Seems all to pieces, what the hell's got you? Wasn't Grimes, surely. He can affect some people. *I* know. Here, let's get you another drink."

"Thanks."

"And try to keep still. Charlie, you're like somebody with St. Vitus's Dance."

"I'm—oh, all right. Yes, I'll have another."

"That's better."

It was.

"I've got somebody in my system, Henge."

And I remember saying it.

"Somebody in your system?"

"Baines," I said.

"Name's common enough, Charlie. How're you feeling now?"

"All right."

"*Sure?*"

"Sure."

"Nice drop of ale."

"Nice."

"You're certain you're O.K.? Still look on the pale side to me."

"The air couldn't get in, couldn't get the window open. I did *try*."

"Now you're off again. Please, Charlie, do try to control yourself. There! That's better. Like a brandy? Might have thought of that in the first place."

"*I am quite all right*. Thank you."

"Right then. Tell me, how did you make out with the old boy?"

"He certainly asked me a hell of a lot of questions."

"Such as?"

"All about my life, found every nook and cranny, climbed in, looked around——"

"Grimes is always very curious about people, Charlie, especially those he employs."

"*Is* he? Well! Well!"

"When you get to know him well, you find a great big father inside."

"Just fancy that."

"Why the hell you ever elected to come and work in a dump like this, heaven only knows."

"I'm a bit odd, I know. I *do* like doing things on the spur of the moment. Mother used to tell me that they left her feeling quite helpless sometimes."

"In the end, Charlie, it depends on how sharp the spur *is*. See what I mean?"

"Beginning to."

"Sure you wouldn't like that brandy? You still look on the pale side to me. You're dead sure you're not ill, got something coming on."

"Of course I am."

"Parts of people get lost sometimes, Charlie. Did you know that?"

"No, I didn't. Heavens! The questions that man asked me," I said.

"Questions. All about what?"

"My life, about Mother. He didn't ask me about the colour of her eyes."

"Where *is* your father, anyhow?"

"He's the one with the answer."

"Like that, is it?"

"Has been for a long time," I said.

"I know this bloody town is over-crowded, *very*. In the road where I live everything except the lavatory has a bed in it. Why didn't you try going to the police? At least you'd have got a cell for the night, and they nearly always manage to land you a pot of tea."

"Who goes to the police these days?"

"Who does? See your point, Charlie."

"Only one decent hotel in this town," I said.

"*And* it's always packed. People do sometimes come in from a more ugly town to a less ugly one, just for a change."

"I *had* booked——"

"Yes, but *one* night, what's that to-day? They forget fugitives."

"I'm learning bit by bit," I said.

Henge is real, a hard fact, I hang on. Not a sound in this house. I have been on my back for an hour. Of what is the parrot thinking? What does the Baines tribe think, wooden inside the frames, staring down at Winifred's closed eyes? I can hear the draught in the hall, an east wind perhaps. What is more silent than silent? I wonder. I opened wide my eyes, looked at facts. How that wardrobe had beckoned me, how I had torn open the drawers, pulled out my things, one after another, shot them into my suitcase. Is it still there? Packed? I strain on the iron bed, look over. Still there, waiting for me. And I am waiting for them.

I said, "I'll go *now*, this very minute," and I didn't.

I said, "Perhaps to-morrow night I'll get some sleep." Hoping.

I said, "They fascinate, and they bore me, *very* stiff."

And I am still here, waiting. I'm staring up at brown stains on a ceiling, glancing across at a window that will soon be shut again. The bed next door is so huge, so strong, its very gesture, and it *has* a gesture, that a strength of wall gives, can be seen through. Mrs. Baines's kingdom. Baines rack for the hidden hammers, and the nails. The creak still lives in my ears. I can see the room, so very clearly, the small, dynamic, restless room, and in every corner there must lie the weight and wreck of words. Why should I not think of the Book, saviour and spell, anvil and purpose, cry and dream. The thunder outside is an old storm, the flying feet, the multitudes of opening doors, the hearths waiting, home from the world.

Is she still dead, anchored, unable to spring, claw the moment that is desperate, the screech stifled? It's in my ears again, the single word, "rise". A dead word, inside a shut mouth. Can *He* see? Is Tom satisfied now?

"Nothing is twice good," she said.

I heard it, remembered it, the afternoon, the half light of a kitchen that raged with fire, insensate fingers tearing at the cheapest cloth, the mad sparks, the ocean of loss. The wall of ignorance, and the very bricks sad.

"Henge," I said.

"Henge."

I knew where I was.

"You'd want some kind of a bed-sitter?"

"All I want is something quiet, Henge, my *own* room, and somewhere around, a bath, a door that shuts, even locks. A window that opens and closes," I said.

"God! It's as bad as that then, is it?"

"Something very like it."

"Chaps in the factories have the best places, some of them whole flats, think of that. And in this same town, Charlie, there's around two hundred and thirty technologists, and they actually have houses."

"Really?"

"I'll look around for you. Ring a friend of mine this evening. He might help."

"Thanks a lot."

"But I still can't understand why you chose the North, Charlie."

"I just wanted to get away, anywhere, at the time. That's all that was important. It was a lucky pin-thrust. I like old Grimes, *and* Greele. I'll get what I want. I know I will."

"What exactly?"

"Stuffed gownsman first, and then the *lot*."

"Wish you luck."

"Thanks."

"And these people, Charlie. Where did you say they worked?"

"Lawlers."

"*That* place. Biggest scab show in the whole town."

I can see him pushing away his glass, looking surprised, hear him saying, "Sounds to me like what the archaeologists would call a good *dig*. Staggers me, really. Never realized there was such a thing as survival. *How* old did you say they were?"

"Fifties, and it's a good guess."

"Good Lord! Another *age*. I thought they'd gone down the holes for good. Only ever met two people of that remote time. Never stopped talking about something they called the Somme. Real relics. You *did* land yourself, didn't you?"

So far Henge has spilled nothing that will make me think him interesting, though something might come out later on.

"Charlie! Tell you what. If you don't really want to go back there, I think I could fix you up, at least for one night. Rough and tumble stuff, but you probably wouldn't mind that, well, *would* you?"

"The old man liked me. Even that was funny."

"How about it?"

"I've left my things there."

"Quick work then. *Three* days."

"It was enough."

"I'm sure it was."

"It's to-morrow and to-morrow I'm thinking about," I said.

"Of *course*."

I can peep out of this prison, all the way to where Henge stood.

"Hope you got enough to eat there."

"They never seemed to stop eating," I said.

"Sounds healthy enough to me, Charlie, that part of it, I mean."

"Have another?"

And how glad he was to have another. Henge is like that. He leans close, smiles, and the rest's simpler than plain fractions. He likes not paying for anything best in life. I stood in that pub, the one that Baines dreaded. I remember I searched around for a man named Scragge, the bête noire. Not a sight of him. He might have made a change, the odd curve in a set design. I remember a noise, and it's still as clear, in this room that is surrounded by silence.

"Who on earth are they, Henge?"

"Told you, technologists."

"Why, of course."

The way they had trooped in, a squad of them, and not a blue suit amongst the lot. How close together they were, six very earnest-looking men, with together heads. And a *set* look, as if they were suddenly on to something very important. The way they noisily plodded towards that counter. Was it to look at George? Perhaps. An odd barman, a most shining pate, and the rest of him quite lost in one of those gorgeous, loose-hanging sweaters, inside which you can put the whole family.

"Strange-looking man."

"Notice his *eyes*?"

"Everybody notices his eyes. Call him the human error round here."

"Hasn't much to say for himself," I said.

"Will it matter, either way?"

"*No!*" I shouted. Everybody turned round.

"By God! You have got it, Charlie."

"I've just got *out*."

"Yes, but——"

"*Away*. From *there*. You'll never understand, Henge."

"I've been in here Saturdays, Charlie, when you couldn't get in this room for technologists."

"What d'you suppose the antics are?"

"Not for anybody's health, I'm sure of that. Queer lot. Never communicate, except amongst themselves. And do they think they're *it*?"

"I'll have that brandy, Henge," I said.

"*Will* you?" Probably shocked him, but why should I pay for everything?

"Can you get anything to eat in this pub?"

196

"Crisps, cheese biscuits."

"*That* all?"

"Hungry?"

"Of course I'm hungry."

"Then why the hell didn't you *say*?"

"Well I *am*."

"D'you mind fish and the other thing?"

"*No.*"

"Right. Just coming up. Thanks, George. Here, Charlie, toss that back. World will thereafter look a different shape. Hope it's the right one."

"Thanks very much, Henge."

"Sure you won't kip in with me to-night?"

"Sure. I told you I was sure."

"Suit yourself. Free country, and all that."

"Let's finish these drinks and go," I said.

I looked at my watch. It was just six o'clock. It made me think of the Baines family, made me remember. And I think of them now. Below, I can hear occasional crashes of coal on to a steel fender, an occasional hissing as the coal burns.

"By the way, do remind me to post that letter. I've had it in my pocket all day. Took me three days to write it."

"Some letter. Shan't forget, Charlie."

"It was chaotic."

"What did you do with yourself in the evenings?"

"Tried to read, wanted to, to study, to make plans. Everybody talked their heads off."

"What about?"

"I can't be bothered," I said.

"Is *that* all?"

"And sleep. You weren't there, Henge."

"And you won't be to-morrow, Charlie, not if I can help it. You seem to have landed yourself in the strangest place."

"They were alive."

"Come on, finish it off, and let's go. I have a home to go to if you haven't, and a nice landlady waiting to say good evening, and a nice hot meal downstairs, and sprawled in front of her telly for as long as I like."

"What's it going to be for you, finally?"

"Me? Well, I hope one more office in Garlston. *My* office. *And* I'll proceed to improve on all the tricks I've been taught. First morning *I* turned in to Greele and Grimes, I had to see the big father, just like you. Tiny man behind a big desk. He was at once dispiriting. Threw open the big safe, looked at me, and said, 'So this is your line then, Henge?' 'What, sir?' I said. 'This,' he said, pointing to a pile of papers inside the safe. 'In that safe, Henge, you will find locked up the town's misery. Misery? Garlston's stumbling footsteps, Garlston's heartbeats, and weaknesses, and greed, and blindness. And I am bound to say, a great deal of stupidity.' "

"A good start," I said, and then, "Are we going?" And we went. Straight out into the street, a crowded street, a noisy one.

"You'll want a bus, Charlie."

"Of course," I said, and I was wanting it, and I was not wanting it, pausing at the kerb's edge, thinking of the voyage out, through the darkness, into the silence, towards Baptist Street, a green back door.

"Why the hell shouldn't I go to the front door."

"What's that?"

"Sorry for talking out loud," I said, more astonished than him.

I remembered that also. In this small room, refused by Winifred, too close to Mrs. Baines's chamber of death for Tom. No sound of the feet, no key in the front door, final signal of the day's end. The light has gone, a sky blackening, the air colder. I got up and closed the window. It made me think of the fire below, a suddenly open door, the warmth enfolding.

Why don't they come? Has something happened? Twenty
minutes after six o'clock. I shut my eyes, I called in my mind,
"Henge."

"What, Charlie?"

"Which way do *you* go?"

"Bottom of this road, turn left, cross over, first right, and
there I am. End of a voyage. Always glad to get home."

"No ambitions beyond that office in the town?"

"Nothing beyond that. No horizons."

"Not many left to-day, horizons I mean."

"Not many."

"See you as far as the bus, Charlie."

"Half a minute, your paper?"

"*Evening Blade*. Have it if you like."

"I'll buy one," I said.

"Pity you weren't down here on Sunday, you'd've seen the
big show."

"This the only newspaper in Garlston?"

"Only one. Used to be old Sutcliffe's, and now it's just one
more hinge on a London magnate's golden door. Even *The
Blade* can't make up its mind about the bomb."

"Bugger the bomb."

"Feel like that myself sometimes. But you can't dodge it.
Have to think about it in the end."

"My landlady's husband says there's a bigger, more important bomb than the *bomb*."

"Oh, yes. I haven't heard anything about it, and I read all
the papers, Charlie. What kind?"

"Explosive. Like the rest."

"You know, Charlie, I think you're trying to be funny about
something in which there just isn't any fun."

"I'm sick of the bloody thing. Now, where's that bus?"

"Must have another chat about this," Henge said.

"Must."

Listening again. Was that the parrot? Remembering again, hearing the sound of my own feet, moving towards a bus with Henge. Coming on this suddenly, admiring it. Watching a queue move slowly, dutifully, towards the bus entrance, rain-coated all, against the rain that loves to pour. Faithfully through the drizzle, past the bent conductor, coughing into one hand. The raincoats touched each other, made little spitting sounds. I loved the orange of the vehicle, so bright. On moving, it will burst into flames.

"Garlston has a nice colour sense," I said. "Certainly likes bright colours."

"Do *you*?" And rather snappily, I thought.

Had Henge drunk too much? Too little?

"I feel sure you were——" paused, and Henge said, "I was what?"

I saw Henge near, and I saw him somewhere in a middle distance, another Henge. Black-bearded, duffle-coated, the glasses to his eyes, as he searched in a dim mist for the horizon that refused to come up. A strong head wind, and the ship carrying a list of forty degrees. And then I shot.

"Destroyers?"

"Good Lord! How'd you guess, Charlie?"

"Knew you were Navy."

"That's right," Henge said, and then added, as if quoting, "and then all the days were tame."

"Don't you find this sort of thing dull—I mean after *that*?"

"Dull!"

I thought he'd laugh his head off. Is he very easily amused?

"You've only just got here, Charlie. And when you've had it as long as I have, you'll get right behind what's dull. Raise your eyebrows for you."

"What time's the next bus?"

"Ten minutes."

"Shall we?"

The Brown Cow was full of wet people, but Henge navigated well.

"A month here, Charlie, and you'll just be one of us."

"Thanks for telling me."

Something like a small explosion in front of the bus, and then we were off, and through a fugged window I saw Henge waving. We sailed through a river of rain, into an avenue of blinking lights. Towards Baptist Street, and no change. The colour of the Baineses' front door will always be the same. Have they ever noticed it? Perhaps not.

"Getting damned chilly up here," I thought, and I got up and shut the window. I can't help thinking about the Baines family. I've been so close to them these last three days, like skin. Nor can I help wondering where they are, now, in this very moment. On their way home? On which road? Is she very close beside him? If I shut tight my eyes the vision is clearer. And I waited for the feet, and the halt, and the key, and the voice of Baines. "Sright." Shall I go down now. Sit by that fire? Is the hall silence too intense to break, Winifred's door too tightly shut? Are the Baines pair upright? How fast do they walk, how slow? So close together, so very close. Wet in their overcoats, plodding home? Was that the parrot *again*? Will they never come? Has something happened? Is it too much? Does Baines, who doesn't mind, mind now?

The open drawers of the big wardrobe gape, like mouths. One could sleep comfortably in a drawer, snug. How bright it is in a dark room, and of solid oak. How did they get it upstairs, get it inside? I talked to myself, again, in the absence of anything else.

"Go down now."

"I think I will."

"But there's nobody *there*."

"The kitchen's warmer than this."

"Is Winifred dead?"

And suddenly a man named Crawley was growing, right through the silence. I thought about Crawley. Mysterious, remote, perhaps powerful. Tall or small? Thin or fat? Does he, too, wear a blue suit? Thinking of him, I am bound to think of Joshua. Has it happened? Has "the fall" suddenly appeared to Baines, black cloud over his grey bench, over the glittering nails? Has he felt the push behind him, has she? Baines is huge at his bench, but Crawley grows, obscures the vision. *Did* it happen? Is dread still creeping up the Baines back? Has she heard the feet, "terrible feet, Mr. B.," tramping in her ears. Has Crawley, too, felt a push in the back? From his new wife, snug at Lovedene? Has Crawley had his senses rocked by sense more common? Heard her talking in his ear about shares? Has he felt her teeth in his neck. "Economise, John. Sack them." Has Crawley heard?

The clock struck seven, the echo thudded.

"But if Crawley did, Mr. B. If he did——"

"Pray, Mrs. B."

I lit another cigarette, thought about going down. And suddenly I was sitting up, thinking about it. I got up, moved slowly round the room, picked up things and put them down again, sat again and studiously studied the carpet strip, walked to the window, opened it again, noticed the grime for the first time, even a flocculence. Perhaps Tom stood here, looked out through a closed window, heard Mrs. Baines move elephant-like in the next room. The darkness is complete, the rain came down. Drops spat down the chimney, the green paint of the tiny grate looked grease-like. I stood at the door, fiddled with the loose knob, saw where a tiny bolt had been. I peeped out, and the air was colder. The linoleum shone its green all the way down the stairs. The tiny fanlight seemed moving in the darkness. And at that moment I heard the feet, unmistakable. "They'll come in through the back door."

"The front one."

"No. The front one is for Sundays," and it made me think of *next* Sunday, Tom waiting, and Winifred going, sailing through her fantastic dream, the will-less one behind, a hand heavy on his arm. I heard the back door unlocked. The slow steps across the yard. I thought of the shed, "the den". Will he go out there this evening, brood there, without the lamp? Will he pick up his flute? Play? Will she come straight upstairs, pause at the bottom, listening for the sounds, the very heavy breathing of "that one". A sudden halt.

"You'd better go down now, Charlie," I said.

"They'll be soaked to the skin."

"They love walking," I said.

"In her big hand she can clutch a penny tighter than anybody."

The keys to the kingdom rattle, the door shrieks, the door shuts.

I stood at the top of the stairs, listening.

"Nobody here, Mr. B."

"Sright, but it's funny, Mrs. B."

"Funny?"

"I mean odd then."

"That one's done nothing, Bainesy, nothing."

"I know, Mrs. B. I can see. Have eyes."

And like a gunshot, acid in the bullet, "Have you, Mr. B.?"

At what is Baines staring? The remains of his breakfast? At what is she? The faithful fire?

"Must be asleep."

"Must be."

"Feed her, Bainesy."

"Very well."

"The least thing you could expect that one to do is earn her keep."

No answer.

203

"I'm talking to you, Mr. B."

"I know."

"Then have you nothing to say then, nothing?"

"Nothing, Mrs. B., nothing," and the voice, deep, and right down in his boots.

"Come, dear," I heard Baines say.

The parrot communications seem conspiratorial, low in a parrot throat. What does she say? Talking about the silence? Being lonely all day? That one never coming to see her, even the once, and no food.

"S'starving, Mrs. B.," Baines said.

"We are all starving. And where's he, I wonder?"

"Who then?"

"And who'd you think?"

"Ah," Baines said, "ah," velvet soft to the bird. Make a hole anywhere in Joshua and kindness oozes out.

"Funny Charlie's not here, Mr. B."

"Lawlers are not the only ones, Mrs. B., others work overtime too."

"Don't you ever mention that name to me again, Bainesy, d'you hear?"

"I hear."

"Glad you do."

"Now I'll clear this mess up. I shan't be disturbing *that* one, thank you."

The crash of the back kitchen door should have waked the dead, but it didn't.

"You ought to be glad you're a bird, Polly," Baines said, the words like fingers, stroking. "Ah! You're enjoying your bit of grub. Nice din dins for the nice bird. Ah——" the final stroke, real plush.

"Mr. B."

"S'll be dreaming again soon, Polly, expect, wish I was you, really," Joshua said.

"Bain*sey*!" roared Mrs. Baines.

"Coming, Mrs. B."

"About time. Are you *dream*ing? Hope to God not, Bainesy. Your days for dreaming are almost over."

"I know what my days are, Mrs. B."

And Baines clumps, from one room to another, perhaps not even hearing the heavy treads, perhaps not caring. Where is the load heaviest?

"There! Sit down."

"Thought that rain'd never stop coming."

"Being with you, Bainesy, I thought the same myself."

"Shall we——?"

"We shan't then, Mr. B. We'll wait for him."

"Very well."

"I'd better go and change this dress."

"You better had."

I went in again, stood behind the door.

"I must go down now," I thought, not going. I heard Mrs. Baines come up. She reached the top.

"Oh, God!" she exclaimed, and closed her door.

"It *can't* have happened. Impossible. No. No. Not after all those years of faithful work? Surely not. The *end*? Unbelievable. Is Baines hunched, heavy in his chair? Is Baines hoping? Is he thinking of the dream, the voice in his ear, the house talking?

"You should get up, Mr. Baines."

I can almost hear it myself. Heavy breathing in the next room.

The door again, opened, closed, the feet down the stairs, and *another* door. Banged. I sat down on the bed again. Tomorrow I'll be gone.

"He's very late."

"He won't be long."

"You haven't been to see if she——"

"No, I haven't."

"I went out there, Mrs. B., couldn't even hear her breathing, sort of."

"Sort of *what?*"

A Lawler nail accidentally slipping into Mrs. Baines's throat.

"Very still," Joshua said.

"She'll be huddled, Bainesy, make no mistake about that. Sometimes she's in there so *long*, I think she's like one of them animals as feeds on itself."

"What are you talking *about*, Mrs. B.?"

"Her."

"Then leave her, then leave her be," Joshua said.

"He just hinted and no more, Bainesy? Crawley, I mean."

"S'all."

"Did you bow then, Bainesy, say Ta very much, you're quite capable of anything."

"I said nothing at all to that, Mrs. B."

"Sometimes that's even worse."

"I'll make some tea."

"Perhaps you had."

"Saw a bit of cold stuff out back as'll do me."

"He's very late, Bainesy."

"Shall we then?"

"Wait a bit longer then."

"Very well."

"He *is* going?"

"In the morning. Said it to me straight last night."

"I'll miss the money."

"I know, but something'll come along, I'm sure of that."

"Sure of everything, aren't you? D'you think he'll come, that Crawley, *do* you, dressed up as Father Christmas? Sometimes, Mr. B., you make me feel ill."

"He wouldn't be up in his room, Mrs. B., d'you suppose?"

"Go and see then."

"I will."

And Baines came up slowly, and I stood just within the door. He reached it, he knocked. The breathing is engine-like. I waited. He knocked again.

"Yes?"

"Ah!" he said. "Ah! S'wondering where on earth you was, Charlie."

"I'm here."

"I see an' all," he said, and I opened the door.

"Come in, Mr. Baines."

"Ta."

"Sit down."

"Thanks, Charlie," he said, and sat down on my bed. "Ah——!" a great sigh. "S'bin up here long, then?"

Click, and the light was on, and heavily on Baines, blue-eyed, staring. Is Baines grey, greyer than yesterday? Do I notice anything about the total frame? The great hands lie clasped on his knees. His hair is wet, his collar holds on to what seems left of the tie, a piece of blue string.

"S'got the hint to-day," he said.

"The hint?"

"Aye," he said, and the word had the weight of a paving-stone.

"I don't understand, Mr. Baines."

"S'what I was telling you about t'other night, Charlie, that Crawley."

"Oh, *him*."

"Sright. S'up to there, she's right up, ah, I was sorry for her, I'll tell you," and he put a finger on his neck.

"Who?"

"Mrs. B. Her slumped soon's I told her about it. Way she dreads it, wouldn't understand of course, you wouldn't, Charlie. A different world yours."

"I suppose it is."

"Ah——!" and he made no attempt to rise, but sat on, looking at me, and I wondered what he was thinking.

"S'bin up here some time then, Charlie?"

"About an hour."

"Ah——!"

"You're late this evening," I said.

"Ah——!"

"Very late, it's turned seven o'clock, Mr. Baines."

"Ah——!"

"I must have fallen asleep," I said.

"Did you then?"

"Think I was dreaming, really. I kept dozing, waking up again. I must go down. I don't want to keep Mrs. Baines waiting."

"Sright. Time you were gone on down there. Supper's ready, nearly."

Even his voice is grey.

"Awful weather," I said.

"S'horrible. We got soaked."

"I did myself."

"Didn't hear her then?"

"Hear who?"

"Our Winifred."

"Not a sound, Mr. Baines. Probably asleep."

"Wonder though," he said, and then rose to his great height. "Sometimes she'll save something up inside her, Charlie, s'like a bit of spite, really, won't do nothing for nobody, not even herself."

"I understand. A pity," I said.

He turned to the door. "Won't be long then. Mrs. B. hates waiting."

"Shan't be long."

"Ta then," and he moved at last, so slowly, his feet leaden, the fingers pulling irritatedly at the cloth of his trousers, and then he paused at the door.

"Won't say anything to her then?"

"I shan't say a word about anything, Mr. Baines."

"Sright then," and out he went.

I remained standing on the top stair. I heard her speak.

"Well then?"

I knew she was standing at the foot of the stairs, and it was too dark for her ever to have seen me.

"Up there all the time, Mrs. B. Says he's bin in an hour, s'fell asleep he says, dreaming."

"Fancy that then."

"Ah——!"

"Stir up that fire, Mr. B."

I heard the flames roar.

"Is he coming or isn't he then?"

"S'coming, don't fuss, Mrs. B., s'not the time for fussing about little things to-day. You know that s'well as I do. Big things too close, *too* close."

"Get sat then, Bainesy," she said.

"I am sat."

"Shan't be long then."

"Ah——!"

"You do sound tired to-day, Bainesy, s'all right, I hope. Not ill?"

"Not ill."

"I'm glad."

"*He* never heard a sound from out there neither, says she's probably asleep."

"Bit of quiet'll be a change then," Mrs. Baines said.

"Aye. Just leave her be."

"I'm *leaving* her be."

"No need to shout then, Mrs. B. God! I'm sort of heaving up inside me to-day."

"Think of him, Bainesy, that Crawley, no more'n the height of two chamber pots, 'n him having the power to tell us which'll be our black day, and which won't. Think of that then." She paused, then added, "Feel a bit sick myself, though I don't shout about these things."

"Course you don't. You don't grumble at all much, and what bit you does I manage to put away tidy, forget it. Have to."

"Suppose it *does* happen, Bainesy?"

"Suppose it doesn't."

"Crawley's a bastard, Mr. B., and I could call him worse names."

"But we shall not kneel to a bastard, shall we?"

"We shall not."

"Ah! Here you are then," Baines said.

They were seated at the table. She looked up as I entered, but did not speak. I saw the Book lying open in front of Joshua. For a moment I felt I had pried into something intimate, terribly private. Baines did not look up, but concentrated on the Book, turning over its pages one after the other. Was Crawley upright in their minds, ready to crush?

"Good evening, Mrs. Baines."

No reply, but her hand waved me to the table. I sat down.

"Awful weather."

No answer.

And the words that were lighter than her own breath. "You are leaving then?"

"I am. First thing in the morning," I said.

"Was it——?"

"It wasn't, and it isn't anything," I said.

"Do I say *Ta* for what you've said then?"

She swung round and looked down at me. It seemed as if

for the first time I saw her total, final. The frown, and the brow that is immense, the uplifted arms that could hold up the house, the eyes that watch Baines, and now watched me.

"I'm just going, Mrs. Baines," I said, very quietly, "that's all."

"Go then."

"I have to be near my work."

"I'm sure you do."

When I looked at Baines I thought of the lighthouse without lights. Suddenly he laid the flat of his hands across the pages of the Book. The head was erect, the eyes shut. The hands began slowly to close as if grasping the words beneath them. I glanced at Mrs. Baines.

"Do I owe you anything, Mrs. Baines?"

"*Nothing.*"

For what are we waiting? When shall we begin to eat?

I waited, and I looked round, *and* round. Of what is the parrot thinking? The wooden eagle atop the dresser seems to peck unmercifully at Joshua's blue scarf. The teapot that is ageless sits on a hot hob. The silence seemed too sudden. I must look beyond this, beyond them, bore through the wall, watch Winifred, bent or stretched, or curled, and in the moment, abandoned. I must watch the plant, fantastically green, burdened by its own weight of foliage, still reaching for the ceiling, climbing, and yet climbing. What level of air does it seek? The polar bed, and the burden on it. The seat in the window, worn, and the curtain that half drapes its back. Is it still warm, and what did she see, at the last moment, before she reached for the bed, friend and saviour? Did the moment collapse with a thud? The wooden faces upon the wall, fixed in time? The door that bears the rub of shoulder and frame?

"Charlie's hungry, Mr. B. I suppose you know *that?*"

The Word draws Baines down, and down. He will not look up.

"We are all hungry," Baines said.

"Go on, go on then, Bainesy, *do go on*."

"Your mouth seems always open to me, Mrs. Baines," Joshua said, and slowly he raised his head, looked first at his wife, and then at me.

Then the voice, that was with angels and with bells.

"Is there not a warfare to man upon earth?
And are not his days like the days of a hireling?
As a servant that earnestly desireth the shadow,
And as a hireling that looketh for his wages:
So am I made to possess months of vanity,
And wearisome nights are appointed to me.
When I lie down, I say,
'When shall I arise?' but the night is long;
And I am full of tossings to and fro unto the dawning of
    the day.
My flesh is clothed with worms and clods of dust;
My skin closeth up and breaketh out afresh.
My days are swifter than a weaver's shuttle,
And are spent without hope.
Oh!—remember that my life is Wind."

"Amen," Mrs. Baines said.

"Amen," I said, having to.

It seemed then as if Winifred had dropped words into my ear.

"I shall fall no further, Charlie."

"*Eat,*" Joshua said, and I ate.

He suddenly paused, raised the spoon in the air.

"Shall we——" pausing, hesitant in a moment, uncertain, looking at her, wondering.

"Shall we what then, Mr. B.?"

"Shall we call her?"

"That one may come in when we are gone, Mr. B. Get on with it then."

"I am getting on."

"Then *get* on then."

"You are not full up yet, Charlie," she exclaimed, "*surely*?"

"Nearly, Mrs. Baines, nearly," I said, "thank you."

"In this life, Charlie," announced Joshua, "there is nothing like a friend."

And then I had had enough. My shout was wholly unexpected.

"I'm not hungry. I never *was*. I *mean* it."

And then I laughed. I had to, and I couldn't stop. It got louder and louder. Mrs. Baines gripped her knife, Baines dropped his own.

"*Charlie!*"

Suddenly Mrs. Baines jumped to her feet, rushed to the door, and went out, slamming it behind her.

"Stop *laughing*."

"I *can't*."

"*Charlie!* D'you hear me then, do you?"

He rose majestically, came round to me, gripped my arms. "Stop!"

And I couldn't stop. The Book closed with a snap. Baines suddenly drew away from me. And I went on laughing.

"You've suddenly gone *mad*, Charlie, that's what."

I didn't even look at him, and when for the second time the kitchen door slammed, I knew that he too had departed. And I sat at their table, and I could *not* stop laughing.

"I can't *stand* it," and I too rushed out of the kitchen. For a moment I stood transfixed in their green hall. I heard their bedroom door close. Then slowly I mounted the stairs. I was no more than half way up when I heard the voice behind me, and when I turned, there was Winifred.

"*Mind* you," she shouted, and seemed to hurl herself up the remaining stairs.

For a moment I was too astonished to speak.

"I thought *you* were *dead*."

"I'm not."

She was already hammering on their bedroom door.

"*I* heard you at it, the lot of you. I *know*. What did you tell him about me? You *bitch*, you been saying things to Charlie about *me*," and the voice leapt for a top note. "About *me*! Listen to him now, *listen*, he can't stop laughing."

And she continued to hammer on the wall. I did manage to reach my own room, got in, and quickly shut the door. And then I shouted at the top of my voice, "I've had *enough*!" I began collecting my things, hat, coat, case, scarf. The drumming on the door continued. Winifred was desperate.

"You told lies about me, both of you, you *did*, but Charlie's more clever than you lot. More clever, I *said* it, you bitch. It's you, it's always bloody you. *He* knows. *I'm* not mad, I never was. It's *you*, and that great dog you have crawling at your heels—you—you——"

The silence was momentary.

"He's gone into his room. You can hear me, I can see you in there, both of you, hiding. You're always hiding when you're not leaning on God Almighty himself. He is *going*. He told me. It's you, you want everything in this house, everything, don't you, then——"

There was a frantic call from Baines.

"*Charlie!*"

I didn't answer. "God," I thought, "the sooner I'm out of this, the better."

"*Charlie!*"

Joshua burst into my room, clutched my arms, fell on one

knee. "Wait! Just a minute then, Charlie. Wait then. Don't take any notice of her." He looked up at me, and added in a just audible whisper, "Don't go then."

"But I *must*——"

"Ah——!" he said. "Ah! S'first one as ever talked to me, Charlie, as ever sat with me out there, fact, Charlie, fact."

A pause, and then, "I was so glad of that, Charlie."

There was a frantic screech outside, and I knew it was Winifred.

"You great bitch, you kill *everybody*—you—you——" and the words locked in the throat, refusing to come out.

The next moment she too had burst into my room. It was now *full*.

"Charlie, Charlie, tell me then, what were you laughing at, *please* then? I'm not mad, am I? You know. You're cleverer than that lot. Say it, Charlie, say it," and I am drowned in Baineses.

"Wait then, Charlie, a *min*——" and Baines holding on, and on.

"Am I, Charlie?" Winifred said.

And I said, "*Please*. For the love of *God*!"

And I pushed my way out.

I tore down the stairs, and she tore after me. Behind her Joshua's footsteps might have been boulders falling into the sea.

Is Mrs. Baines stood rock-like behind that door? Have the words died in her mouth? Has Crawley enveloped her?

"Don't go then, Charlie," Baines said, "not yet."

And Winifred screeched, "He *is* going."

At the bottom of the stairs I turned, I had to. There was something sad, pathetic about Winifred.

"Where'll you go then, Charlie?" she asked.

"*Out!* Where else? You're all——"

I looked at Baines, and he looked at me. He had sat down

heavily on the bottom stair. In the green hall there was the tiniest sound.

"Ch—Ch——" Baines said.

I am clutched by Winifred, the hands throb on my arms. *"Tell* me."

"You are not mad."

As I put my hand on the latch, I heard for the first time the voice of Mrs. Baines, and it thundered down the stairs.

"Leave him be, Bainesy, just leave him be then."

Baines is only a heap on the stairs, but Winifred is a leech. *"Charlie!"*

"Please!"

"Am I——?"

"You are *Not*," I said, and flung open the door, and the moment it did so, her hands fell, and then she made a mad rush into the parlour and banged the door. I hardly realized it for a moment, but I was *out*. Quietly I shut the door. Quietly I walked into the length, the seeming endlessness of Baptist Street. And as I walked the voices beat in my ear, loud and distinctive, one after the other.

"I'll often think of you, Winifred," I said. "Wonder how things are getting on, what you're doing——"

And the voice that is clearer than my own.

"I'll just be going on then, Charlie, s'usual, living, I suppose."

"I suppose so."

"Charlie!"

"And Mr. Baines?"

"Oh well, then, he'll just go on not minding, I suppose. That's all."

But it wasn't, for Winifred's voice dies under the weight of Joshua's.

"I'll be up every morning, Charlie, nails won't wait, they never does. Mrs. B.'ll be up too, feed her bird, have our breakfast, then us off together *again*, that's it, Charlie."

216

And it was, and it will be, forever and forever.

I paused in the middle of Baptist Street, but only for a moment.

For an instant I imagine them barring my path. These people blaze, but there is no way in between the flames.

When I reached the bottom of the street, I stopped again.

"*Out*," I thought. "Out," I said.

And I walked slowly back, *in*to the world.

JAMES HANLEY

AN END AND A BEGINNING

A Novel of the "Fury" family

"He is among the half dozen most mature craftsmen working in the English language. . . . It is a book dark with dense emotions, full of pity and understanding of the human heart."
—KENNETH ALLSOP (*Daily Mail*).

"*An End and a Beginning* is not a novel to be summed up in a facile sentence—the intensity of Mr. Hanley's vision forbids it."—*Times*.

"Dostoievskian in theme and stature. It is grim and powerful, moving as inexorably as fate to its predestined end. Yet, despite its grimness, it has flashes of sheer poetry."—FRED URQUHART (*Time and Tide*).

"Deeply felt and compassionate. . . . Inspired by this writer's highly individual feeling for his fellow men . . . a warmth of human relationships, concentrated here on the man emerging from a fifteen-year prison sentence for killing the moneylender who is persecuting his mother . . . moving and powerful."
—VERNON FANE (*Sphere*).

"Vast and grand and serious. . . . The pictures of women show a further extension of James Hanley's sensibility."
—JOHN BETJEMAN (*Daily Telegraph*).

THE CLOSED HARBOUR

A Novel

"The quality of its writing, the concentration of its narrative, its deep insight into the splendours and miseries of marine life, make it never less than remarkable."—*The Times Literary Supplement*.

"He is a proved master of his craft . . . his originality and effortless power when posing the figures of tragic drama on earth's stage mark him clear of all contemporaries."—H. M. TOMLINSON (*The Seafarer*).

"A tense and glorious book, full of poetry, pity and humour."—GEORGE D. PAINTER (*New Statesman and Nation*).

"This is one of Mr. Hanley's best novels . . . maintains its force and driving power from beginning to end."—C. P. SNOW (*Sunday Times*).

"Stark realism, compassion and unsurpassed knowledge of those who go down to the sea in ships."—*Birmingham Post*.

"There is something quite incomparable about the sea fiction of James Hanley. . . . This book will certainly enhance Mr. Hanley's very considerable reputation."—ALASTAIR MACRAE (*Evening Citizen*).

A BOOK SOCIETY RECOMMENDATION

LEVINE

A Novel

"A novel that is brilliantly organised, compassionately and beautifully written . . . it has a mounting intensity, a pitiless awareness of the details that turn a desirable proximity into a hateful one. Most of all, *Levine* deals, in prose that is always finely balanced, with a crucial theme, one which Mr. Hanley pursues to a bitter, dramatic end, the incompatibility between love and freedom."—*The Times Literary Supplement.*

"James Hanley is at his best in *Levine*, and for the many readers who know his work no more need be said."—M. R. RIDLEY (*Daily Telegraph*).

"As satisfying a novel as any he has yet written."—*Punch.*

"The dramatic forcefulness of *Levine* creates an impression so sharp that the feel of it lingers after the novel is read. This is James Hanley in his most realistic mood, a writer who reveals with a remarkable economy of phrase the pathos behind the horror of human tragedies of character and circumstance . . . a powerful and moving book."—*The Scotsman.*

"This assured and technically brilliant novel."—*The Tablet.*

"Drawn with a masterly hand in strong outlines and deep colours."—LETTICE COOPER (*Yorkshire Post*).

DON QUIXOTE DROWNED

Studies of Sailors, the Sea and of life in the Welsh Hills

"Reflections of such vitality that they have transferred their existence to the printed page . . . too good to be missed." —GUY RAMSEY (*Daily Telegraph*).

"A mature writer with a poet's feeling, and the fusion of these qualities with his own experience has given him that wonderful and deceptive readability which is achieved only by the first rate."—MARGARET LANE (*Observer*).

"James Hanley is among those few virile writers who by single-minded devotion to their own vision have navigated the treacherous seas of post-Joyce fiction to find themselves esteemed as the most important living exponents of their craft."—EMYR HUMPHREYS (*Sunday Times*).

"Gave me an extreme pleasure . . . I do not know whether literary prizes and dignities are showered upon James Hanley, but they ought to be; and two such triumphs as *Don Quixote Drowned* and *The Anatomy of Llangwyllch* should speed their coming."—OLIVER STONOR (*John O'London's*).

"A writer who wrestles with the stubborn stuff of life and looks deeply into its heart."—*Manchester Guardian*.